scuffler

scuffler

harvey orkin

Harcourt Brace Jovanovich
New York and London

Printed in the United States of America

Library of Congress Cataloging in Publication Data
Orkin, Harvey.
    Scuffler.
    I. Title.
PZ4.0713Sc   [PS3565.R55]   813'.5'4   74-12270
ISBN 0-15-179700-5

First edition
B C D E

for gisella,
jenna,
and
anthony

"a fake
diamond
is a real
something"
—big jack fleedhurn

Women's Lib, Black Lib, Gay Lib, what about Me Lib? Yes, me, Tod Fleedhurn, not a group, not a class, just one human being but all of that, and you'd better remember it. At least I will be when everybody stops trying to mastermind me. I'm goddam sick and tired of being mastermound. Because I'm seventy-two years old, been a hell-raiser all that time, and if I had my life to live over again I wouldn't change a thing. Oh, maybe I'd part my hair on the other side but that's all. Been in and out of jail twice and in and out of love a half-dozen times, or maybe the other way around. And from now on whatever I do, I want to know I'm the one doing it and I want you to know it. I want . . . Hell, I live in want. Me with $84,000,000 in my own name and number (Swiss bank). Ah hah, now you're listening. Bring me another Scotch and milk, Leroy.

Because if you don't listen to people, how're you going to learn? I guess you listen to everybody and then make up your own mind; but that's the hard part. Back when I was a kid, thirteen years old on the farm outside Rapid City, South Dakota, my dad, Big Jack Fleedhurn, took me aside one day and said, "Tod, my boy, are you smoking cigarettes back of the barn?"

"No, I'm not, Pop. No dreaded week for yours truly."
I always told my father the truth.

He shook his head and smiled a little. "Son of
mine," he said, "I'd rather you smoked a hunnert
cigarettes in the house and told me the truth than one
behind the barn and lied about it. A lie is the wust
thing they is." He opened a pack of Sweet Caporals,
put them on the table, and said, "There'll always be an
open pack for you here, son. Hold your head high and
smoke in the house."

I lit right up and have been smoking ever since.
When I tell you that this was the best advice Big Jack
ever gave me, you can figure out how good the rest of
his guidance was.

O.K. He died about two years later and our
mom—there was just my brother, Little Jack, and
me—she married a pharmaceutical salesman and they
went to live in Madison, Wisconsin. She always did
like the bright lights. No offense. So Little Jack, who
was then, as he is now, four years older than me, and I
went into town, Rapid City, as I said before, where we
sought and found employment at the Chateau Pool
Hall and Steam Bath Emporium. It was the time of my
life. Because I still didn't know what I was doing. Get
the picture?

"Hey, kid, you want to brush off the tables?" Little
Jack would say every morning, making me do what he
wanted by the question method so favored by the late,
great Socrates, many years earlier of course.

"Bet I do, Jack."

"How's about a beer, kid?"

"Great." He'd open a couple bottles of beer and we'd
light up and while I'd finish the tables and then post
the morning lines in the back on the tracks around the
country, we'd talk—the kind of talk a guy's got to
have.

"Someday, kid, we're going to have a store all our own. In a city, a real city."

"Maybe St. Louis, eh, Jack?"

"Maybe even Pittsburgh."

"My God."

"It won't be small-time like this. We'll have a Bar and Grill, take bets on the gee-gees, have snooker in the front and craps in the back, whatever anybody wants. And someday, someday in this great country of ours, men will be able to bet, not only on the horses, not only on the fights, but on baseball, on football, on basketball, on anything. And no man will leave our place unsatisfied, especially us."

"You've got vision, Little Jack."

"We'll have all that, a kind of All-Purpose Sporting Emporium. We can run in a clean girl or two, in case some of our customers want sex instead of gambling, once in a while. And if some of those Mississippi Dixieland horn players wander in and need muggles, hell, we can give 'em that too. A full Public Service Enterprise."

Just two guys and a dream. Little Jack was always full of ideas. He was really my first mentor. I was taking it all in too, but I sure wasn't ready to go on my own yet.

Then suddenly it all turned. WAR! The dread scourge of the hated Hun sweeping Europe, and Jack got drafted and where the hell was I, what was *I* supposed to do?

Good old Little Jack turned me over to a lady named Penelope Ann Partridge, who played the organ at the Tivoli Gardens Movie Palace and had been going with an organ tuner working out of Sioux Falls. As I look back on it now, I figure Little Jack had filled in there himself, so to speak, when the Organ Tuner was on the road. But I didn't know that then, I didn't know anything, all I knew was that Jack knew the Organ

Tuner, who got drafted along with him.

The day they shipped out, Penny Ann dropped by the Chateau Pool Hall and said, "We've both lost something near and dear to us today, Tod. Why don't you come by the Tivoli for the show tonight and then maybe we can go to the Malt Shop afterwards. Would you like that?" When she said "near and dear," etc., her eyes teared up. I learned later that she was a crier but I didn't know anything then, as indicated above, and I said, "That'd be keen, Miss Partridge."

Let me tell you about Penny Ann. I make her at that time no more than a furlong away from thirty, one side or the other, pretty, no make-up at that time of course, the kind other women write off with "She's such a pretty little woman." Which is a big mistake. Because this is the kind that have sneaky good looks and men are always trying to undress them. More later. And they wind up dancing on the graves of the women who wrote them off.

And me? The only experience I had ever had with ladies of the opposite sex was with my cousins, who were scattered all over South Dakota, and all their friends, all of whom I wouldn't even speak to unless I had gloves on, and some Sioux Indian hookers at the neighborhood whorehouse. I never even thought there could be anything in the middle.

All right, now you've got the picture. I did go by the theater that night and saw a movie that had Mary Pickford in it. She thought she was going to die but she didn't. Then Penny Ann met me out front and we did walk towards the Malt Shop. I always liked to go in there because the old guy pulling sodas was Billy Temple and we all had a lot of respect for him because he had killed a man once. He'd been a Peace Officer—in about 1890—and this other guy tried to rob the First National Bank of the Black Hills. You hear people nowadays say things like "I want to make a contract I can live with" and "He killed me on that deal" or "When she left me I died a little bit." You can't die a little bit; death is the only absolute there is. The only way you can really be party to death and know it is to kill somebody. And that's what Billy Temple had done, killed somebody. Not in the bank account where folks now think it all is, but in the old Labonza. The Real Thing. So I always liked to go in there and get a malt and study Billy Temple when he was bending over, scooping, to see if I could learn something, anything, off the top of his silvery head. A lot of good it ever did me, too.

"Toddy, what are you going to order when we get to the Malt Shop?" she asked as we walked down St. Joe Street.

"Anything at all, Miss Partridge."

"No favorites? Nothing you like better than anything else?"

"Gosh, I don't know."

"Well, how would you like a nice steaming cup of hot cocoa?"

"That sounds swell. But, Miss Partridge, we're passing the Malt Shop!"

"With a marshmallow on it? Floating?"

"Gee, that would be swell. But I told Billy Temple we'd . . ."

"Oh, Toddy, will you look at where we are? Right smack in front of my apartment."

"Oh."

"Now wouldn't you like Penny Ann to make you a hot cocoa with her own two tiny hands in her own cozy apartment? Watch out for the screen door, Toddy."

"Oh."

"I know a boy can be lonely when his brother is far away in the army, fighting for his country."

"I just thought . . ."

"These stairs are so dark. Oooh, excuse me. I'm such a clumsy. Anyway, here we are. You may take off your jacket. Yes, I think I do know a little something about loneliness. Now sit ye doon over there on that couch, Toddy. Yes, I have known loneliness."

"What's the matter, Miss Partridge?"

"Oh, just something in my eye, I guess. Now then, who's a hungry little boy and does he want some delicious cinnamon toast with his steaming hot cocoa and floating marshmallow?"

She went into the next room, taking off her coat and talking to me as she went. When she came back in, her hair was down and she was wearing mules with pink feathers on them. Then she went into the kitchen and started hotting things up for me. I followed her to the door.

"Now, Mr. Nosey," she said, "you just sit in there and Penny Ann will get everything ready."

I saw that there were already some cookies put out on a tray and that two cups and saucers were all ready too. She must have planned all this in the morning while Little Jack and the Organ Tuner were in the train still sitting in the station.

Well, to make a short story, in she came with the tray and all the cookies and the cinnamon toast and set it all down on the table in front of the couch. Then after she turned off almost all the lights, because "when a person is interested in other persons a lot, my eyes open wide and the glare can injure them severely," she sat down right next to me on the couch.

"Now isn't this better than any dirty old Malt Shop?"

"It sure is, Miss Partridge; it's swell." While I was lifting up my cocoa, I felt her hip touching mine and I thought I was going to die. And the cup shook.

"Oh, did Penny Ann make your toddy too hot? She's sorry."

As she took the cup from me, her hand touched mine and the next thing I knew her arms were around my arms and we were kissing, which is what I did with my cousins' friends but this time I thought my whole head was coming off. I was thinking that my cousins' friends had not been my friends at all and I was grabbing her like an octopus.

"Oh my dearest darling," she said. Then she took one of my hundred hands, got up from the couch, and started leading me into the other room—the bedroom!

After those kisses, I'd have followed her down the mouth of a cannon. As I told you before, I'd always thought there were only two kinds of women, and yet here was the whole thing homogenizing. I didn't know what to think or do and now we were in the bedroom. There was no light there, just what we got from the lamp in the dim living room.

"Now you go into the bathroom there and take your things off, and when you get back out here, I'll be ready for you," she said. "My darling."

I went into the bathroom as ordered, ready for her already. I was sixteen years old and at that moment not at all sure of getting any older: I thought I was going to die, I was so excited. I took my pants off, though how I got them over that monster I was carrying around at the time I'll never know. My God, what I'd give for that thing one more time now!

I opened the door and there she was lying on the bed all naked like the painting over the bar in Murgatroyd's Bar and Grill. She was so beautiful and her hair was long and her breasts were big and white and she was moving around a little bit. When she saw me she held out her arms and closed her eyes. I ran across the room, leaped for the bed, and while I was in midair, I ejaculated. The cum went all over the wall, and I fell into her arms.

We kissed, we grabbed, and she went all over me like a carpet sweeper and of course I was useless. I had no value to her at all.

"What's the matter, my sweetest?" she asked as soon as she got her tongue back in her mouth.

"I don't know. I just . . ."

"Oh, I know. You get so many girls, the pick of them," she said. "Whenever you want them." She was all over me. I never knew I had so many parts: an ear, an ass, some toes. "With that body, with this . . ."

"Ouch!"

"And this . . ."

"Ouch!"

"You must have laid every girl in town. No wonder you are bored and jaded; empty, if you will."

"Yes, empty."

"They all want you. But I've got you!"

"My God, now what are you doing?"

"Put it in there!"

"PUT WHAT IN WHERE?"

So that went on for a little, me telling her what she wanted to hear, that I was bored with banging, instead of the truth, that I got so little I went crazy too soon. This made her work all the harder to please me so that when she finally did, she was grateful. I guess.

With Penny Ann I started a habit that I've never shook of endowing people with other qualities when I love something about them. I was wild about her casabas. I couldn't think of anything else. Therefore I also believed she was smart, good-natured, tall, short, good, and true: a regular Boy Scout. You can figure out what kind of trouble this nuttiness got me into and yet I still do it. I still make pretty girls smart and bright men honorable.

Penny Ann took over my whole life. She played me like her organ. "Stand up straight, Tod." "Wash everything thoroughly. Who knows where those hands have been?" "Don't you ever think of reading a book?" "Don't Walk On The Floor!"

She'd say, "Tod, you are so lazy. You have a good mind, you should use it. If the Good Lord In His Infinite Wisdom saw fit to give you the tools he has, and you do not use these tools, you are a spiritual embezzler."

"I do so use the tools God gave me."

"Oh, Tod, what am I going to do with you?" And then she'd do it.

All this went on for a while. The only thing that changed was that in the winter I still got hot cocoa but in the summer she switched me to lemonade. We'd go home and while she read letters from her Organ Tuner and cried, I read Little Jack's letters from France and was proud. He was learning a little blanket-rolling and he already knew a lot about dealing seconds, the things an American soldier had to know, so I didn't worry too much about him. When she was through crying, we'd jump into bed and she would tell me what to do with my life. But as soon as I headed in one direction she'd turn me around to another. That woman was impossible to please except in that one area.

"You just don't have any ambition, Tod."

"I do too. I want us to have our own store, Little Jack and me, and I want to get $10,000 by the time I'm thirty. How's that?"

"Oh, baby," she'd sigh. "You don't get anything in this life. You've got to *do* things. You don't get happy, you *do* happy; you don't get a job, you *do* a job."

"Talking about doing a job, Penny Ann, I've got to get back to the Pool Hall."

"Of course you do, but move over here closer to Penny Ann first," and she'd sigh. She always sighed when I lay down close to her. "I've never, never tried to get. I don't ask you for anything, do I? I've never asked anyone for loyalty and certainly I don't expect fidelity."

"You don't? Really, Penny Ann?"

"Of course not. All I want is obedience and I DEMAND THAT. NOW, PUT IT IN THERE!"

I learned a lot from that lady. Used that advice many times over in many different business deals. Whenever I have a choice between two or three propositions, I just look at one and say—"Put it in there!" I would rather make ten mistakes of commission than one of omission, and I am a wealthy man today. I think you know what I'm driving at.

It was a great ride with Penny Ann for two years, but one day she upped the price of the ticket.

She took me to church. It was the one she played the organ in on Sundays, a small but sturdy left-handed church presided over by one of those preachers who think they have something personal going with God and are willing to let you in on the ground floor. Penny Ann was crazy about him. So one Sunday morning she got up and said, "You're going to church with me." I think she felt that her life was in two parts, the body and soul being pulled in different directions.

"Look, Penny Ann," this sixteen-year-old kid named Me said, "I do what I want to do when I want to do it. I am my own man."

"You're going to church with me"—she was pulling her dress up over those crazy casabas as she spoke—"or don't bother to come back here tonight."

"My good blue suit is stained."

"God cares not what you wear. He seeth inside your soul."

The church was about eight miles out of town, just off the road to Deadwood where Wild Bill Hickok had got his final lumps.

We got there real early because Penny Ann had to start warming up her organ. The church was log-cabin style but the wood was polished. The pews were nothing fancy. There were a few brass fixtures around and at the back there was a kind of statue of Himself on the cross with a nice low candle burning at His feet. As if the nails weren't hurting enough. Folks began filing in and just sat quietly, looking at the pulpit high on the wall. Not many children, no men alone. I had the feeling that in this church the women really felt the need so they made their move and brought their menfolk around. Soon there was a full house, I'll say that for it. Penny Ann was having the time of her life beating on the organ, leaning backwards and forwards, and then Father Bob came out and you could see why the women led the way.

There was about six feet of him but he looked taller because he had arranged it so we were all looking up at him, there in the pulpit, and there was a light shining on this wavy blond hair of his. Moved like an athlete, bounding up those stairs, was built like a brick cathedral, with slim hips and wide shoulders, all under a pair of brilliant blue eyes. And what a voice!

"You're all sinners!" he shouted.

"Oh, that's more true today than it ever was." The woman right behind me was sniffling while she gave herself up to Father Bob.

"You're all sinners." He lowered his voice and leaned forward. "Because you're all better than you think you are."

"Are you grateful?" He was louder again.

"No. No." A whole bunch of voices answered, mostly soprano.

"Are you grateful *enough*?"

"Oh, no, Father Bob" went the chorus.

"Look at that color red," and he pointed to a dark, almost maroon hunk of velvet hanging over the pulpit. "Don't say 'what a pretty shade of red,' don't ever let God hear you say that." He lowered his voice again and I could just feel the whole congregation leaning forward to meet him. "You say 'what a miracle! What a mighty miracle that there is such a thing as the color red!!'"

He had them, he owned them now. All of them, men and women, had their eyes fixed on him, following him while he moved back and forth like a gorgeous mongoose. On he went with a bucketload of "whomsoevers" and "followeths" and telling them to give more of themselves just as Penny Ann had laid on me earlier. With that the collection plate started getting passed.

"Have you tried God? You'll find He's a Good Guy." That scared them all, the way he was bringing his Pal in there, right into the church. "Ask Him for what you want and ye will receive. How does He know what you want if you don't ask Him?" They figured He has an unlisted number and only Father Bob has it.

Then he prayed them off and they started filing out. I had to wait around because my Penny Ann played them all out the door on her organ and then she walked by for me at my pew and we went to the door together, hand in hand, where Father Bob was saying farewell to all the marks. The sun seemed to shine on his hair and he looked so damn confident that you felt you were doing the right thing giving him your soul and even your money. He'd know what to do with them both. Then he and Penny Ann and I went back of the church where he had a little apartment for himself, and he poured out three glasses of delicious Northern Spy apple wine.

"Tod, may I talk to you about what you saw today?" Father Bob asked.

"Oh yes, sir," like I had a choice, with Penny Ann there.

"Good," he said. "This fellowship, the Sons and Daughters of Holy Jesus Christ God Almighty, is very simply a group of men and women, people, if you will, who believe that the whole is greater than the sum of its parts. Do you follow me?"

"No."

"Fine," said Father Bob. "He may not be very bright, Penelope Ann, but he is honest and I respect honesty. Look," he said to me. "Take an automobile. It has wheels, a carburetor, seats, and all those other wonderful things. Put 'em all together and you have not only a collection of those things but you also have an automobile, something that does something and is separate and greater on its own. Because it is together! Now do you see?"

"Yes, yes, I do, Father Bob. I see! You have an automobile!"

"Very good, Tod. He's getting smarter, Penelope Ann. Now let's move along. Let us take, for instance, a seventeen-year-old boy. He has eyes, he has arms, a tummy, a penis"—Penny Ann gulped and I noticed the glint of a tear in her eye—"and all that spells a son of Jesus Christ God Almighty. What you do with all these marvels is up to you. Destiny gives you the task, but it is up to you to accomplish it."

"What am I supposed to do?" I felt like there was a huge load of fear on my chest.

"Just attend these meetings, Tod, and listen closely. You were interested, weren't you?"

"Oh yes, sir."

"Sir? I'm just plain Father Bob; that's what everyone calls me. *Of course* you were interested. Because you have curiosity, good old holy curiosity. And curiosity is the only weapon we have against fear."

"Holy fear?"

"Any fear. For instance, if you see a dark cave with a lot of dangerous naked boys in it and are afraid to enter, curiosity will push you in."

"Sir—Father Bob, you've opened up an entire new vista to me as a person." I was glad now that Penny Ann had made me read some books, because I had new words to use.

"And we have no rules, no rules at all, Tod, just the good old Golden Rule. Do unto others as you would have others do unto you."

And that became the rule I did live by until much

later in my life when I got pitched on another religion, psychiatry, and I tried to figure out what happened when a masochist practices the Golden Rule.

So there I was, a member of a group for the first time, SDHJCGA (Sons and Daughters of Holy Jesus Christ God Almighty), and it was quite relaxing because, in spite of what Father Bob said, there were rules and plenty of them. Signs all over the walls in black and white. He said they were only suggestions but you got the idea that if you didn't follow them it was Good-bye, Charlie, Lock the Door, Katy, or you turned into salt.

But I was getting restless. I really couldn't stand all those sweet smiling SDHJCGAs telling me what to do. And we were attracting all the crazies who showed up in the town, so the movement was growing, if that's the way you want to grow. I remember one Sunday we marched right down St. Joe Street to our monthly picnic and afterwards, while I and some other of the younger religious maniacs were cleaning up the paper and all that which the older nuts had left around, I noticed that a lot of them, especially the ladies of the chorus, were sitting on the ground around a young guy who was talking to them. I thought, Why the hell isn't he doing something too, and worked my way over there.

"France must be beautiful, isn't it?" asked one of the women.

"Yes, it surely is, sister," said the young guy.

"I'd like to see the coast of it," said Penny Ann, who was sitting at his feet. "I've never seen the ocean. It must be marvelous."

"Well," and he laughed, "it's not for me."

"Why not?"

"Twenty-one days on a raft. I was chief gunner's

mate on the U.S.S. *New Hampshire* when she got sunk. All I saw was that ocean for three weeks, day and night. No, I've had my fill of that."

"Oh, you poor lad. Have some more cranberry kuchen."

Naturally, I got a lot of guilt about this poor guy floating around at sea while I was having a good old time picking up garbage at nice comfortable picnics. So I ran around grabbing more than my share of the work while they all fed him more than his share of the food and drink. This was the summer of 1918 and I figured they'd sent him back because he'd been wounded bravely defending me. At least the dreaded Boche was not in Rapid City and he was the nearest one to thank.

Then about two months later the SDHJCGA decided to hold a dance for the Fund Against the Hun to raise money to take care of those babies who were always hurling themselves onto German bayonets, according to the German-Americans around Rapid City, and thus getting severely injured in said process. It was going to be a big deal and all the women of the congregation were baking and cooking like little elves and the men were selling tickets and musicians were hired and there was going to be fun, fun, fun, which of course would help the maimed and orphaned of torn Europe. I wanted to lay eight to five at the Pool Hall that none of the proceeds would reach Europe but there were no takers. My assignment for that night was to keep the glasses washed for the punch and keep squeezing oranges for same.

Then the magic night came and after an hour and a half of playing Cinderella, running all over with clean glasses, picking up the used, squeezing oranges for the punch, I sat down for a moment on the edge of the crowd again around the returned naval hero. By this time, Penny Ann and all the ladies were treating him like an oracle, asking him what the world would be like after the war.

"People will have to learn to live with one another," he said with a beatific smile.

"Oh, when he talks like that I could listen to him all day," said one of the ladies.

"He's gorgeous," another one whispered to my Penny Ann, who nodded.

"Don't you think," asked Penny Ann, "that with the successful emergence of the aeroplane, men and women from one land of Europe will quickly and easily visit another? Then they will not want to wage war on one another. I do hope that is so."

"Ah, I'm not sure I have the faith in the aeroplane you have, sister."

"Why not, brother?"

"Twenty-two missions over German lines till I was shot down." He held his arm out crookedly. "I still can't straighten this out completely."

"Oh, you poor darling," said Penny Ann. "Tod, go get Mr. Kerr another drink. His glass is empty."

"I'll get him shit all." I screamed it as I stood up.

"What language!!" "Where did he hear such words, Penny Ann?" "Shame, shame!" the ladies were saying and out of the corner of my eye I saw Father Bob wending his way towards me.

"He's a liar!" I said. "Last week he said he was in the navy and now he says he was an aviator and he's getting points for them both and I'm washing the lousy dishes. He's a liar!"

"Careful, lad," said our Hero, getting up. "I may have to smite thee."

"Come on outside and I'll smite the hell out of you." I felt I had to say it, even though as he stood up I noticed how big he was for the first time.

"What's all this?" said Father Bob.

"Penny Ann's young friend called Mr. James Kerr a liar," said one of the helpful ladies.

"Now, Tod, he is a guest in our house." Father Bob smiled.

"But, Father Bob, he did lie."

"Why don't the two of you shake hands and forget all this."

And Kerr, smiling, extended his poor crooked arm.

"I don't want to shake his hand."

"Then why don't the two of you go outside and discuss it amongst yourselves."

We went outside, back of the Church Hall where I effected an immediate and miraculous cure because after he jabbed me a few times with his left, that right arm straightened out and knocked me on my ass. Just to make sure he was all right, we repeated this a few more times and then went back in. Penny Ann grabbed me right away and led me to a corner, where Father Bob joined us. Penny Ann was wiping the blood off my nose and I was holding ice to my eye.

"Oh, Tod, how could you do this to me?" she said. "Father Bob, I'm so sorry, so ashamed."

"All right, Sister Partridge, I forgive thee. And I forgive thee too, Toddy."

"Forgive me for what, Father Bob?" I suddenly realized I was crying. I remember that like it was yesterday. It wasn't the pain, it was the humiliation of losing. I have felt that same humiliation since then, and I think of the Final Humiliation often now, which figures, at my age and weight. "I was doing all the work and he got out of it by lying."

"Let the Good Lord exact retribution, Tod."

"I was trying to help Him retribute."

But that was a good lesson for me. The White Hats don't always win. Liars and villains don't always suffer and lose. They often win if the Good Guys can't hook off a jab.

Then everything awful happened at once. Morning of November 11 they announce the war is over and that afternoon who shows up but my brother and the Organ Tuner. They had been together the whole war. I had to move out of Penny Ann's apartment while she did her Penelope to the Organ Tuner's Odysseus. I thought that having Little Jack back would make up for that. Well, Little Jack didn't come back alone. He had married a girl named Debbie from New Jersey and even had a job in a hustle called the Guardian Life Assurance Company of North America and she talked about her hair and they joined the Country Club and they had a kid right away. This was a man who had practically created the six-horse round-robin bet in the entire Northwest, a man who had brought layout craps to its finest hour in the Dakotas. And now it was all over for him.

Little Jack wanted me to go into the insurance dodge with him and join the Club and all but I didn't want to belong to anything but myself. At the same time, Penny Ann AND the Organ Tuner were plowing after me to rejoin SDHJCGA and let Father Bob guide my career as either a poolroom hustler or insurance salesman, whatever God said. I thought that maybe Penny Ann had confessed our little slap-and-tickle to the Organ Tuner, because she never forgave him for the war into which he had allowed himself to be drafted. And I guess he picked forgiveness over vengeance, because he was a churchgoer and all that, but I never knew when one day he might think it over and belt me with one of those brass pipes he was always handy to. One night they made me come over and they had Father Bob there and then when the other two went to the movie palace, he made a big pitch at me.

"Why don't you come on God's team, Tod?"

"Oh, God doesn't even know I'm alive, Father Bob."

"His eye is on the sparrow." And Father Bob's hand was on my thigh.

"Tell Him to get it off the sparrow." I tried to shout but it was coming out like a croak because his hand was getting right on the old jewelry. "Because it's this boy who's in trouble."

He gave a grab and a squeeze, I gave a jump and a run, and he fell off the couch.

Next day I got on the bottom of a train leaving for parts west, blowing the town before it could do the same to me.

As we know now, He should never have rested that
seventh day. That's where He cheapened Himself. I
found that out a long time ago, but I've got this sort of
emotional hernia that makes me afraid to believe it.

I rode the rods down to Ogden, Utah, where I picked
up a job cooking for a sheep rancher who had a spread
about one hundred miles out of town. Actually I was
the assistant to the cook, a man named Smith, but you
couldn't call him Smitty or he'd hit you. Listen, all
cooks are crazy, but whether that's why they become
cooks or the cooking makes them that way, I'll never
know, though I do know that you are what you do
anyhow and there's a reason why you started doing it.
All hangmen must have something in common, just
like people becoming lawyers so they can tell other
people what to do or doctors to make sure they will
always be around people worse off than they are.

All cooks have bad dispositions and drink gallons of
coffee, usually out of soup bowls, and often perform
strange rites.

This Smith, for instance, in the middle of winter
would take a bath in the bunkhouse and then get right
into his clothes without drying himself. Never used a
towel. Never talked hardly at all either. Just cooked for

the men on the ranch, not the rancher and his family, and I washed spuds for him, broke eggs for the breakfasts, cleaned up, and all that. Plenty of work. Smitty was the best short-order cook I've ever seen, and he was all right otherwise as long as he was cooking. The other ranch hands stayed away from him because they were smarter than I was, but I got interested in his activities.

For instance, he was having it off with Mrs. Kutcher, the rancher's wife, and also with one of their daughters, Blossom. He had a special door to his room in the bunkhouse and he had that balanced sense of timing you get doing toast and frying eggs and boiling coffee and all that at the same time. I believe he was also boffing one of the sheep, and I think Mr. Kutcher would have had his heart out for that because, as a Mormon, he knew that he could have all the wives he wanted at that time but a good sheep, well, she could lose her coat over this. Anyway, I used to watch the door for him.

Smitty was a terrible gambler, loved playing cards for big stakes. I'm telling you, if the Winter Olympics were played on thin ice, he'd be a Gold Medal Winner hands down.

I was there about three months through that winter, and in all that time I never saw him smile once and I never heard him laugh. He didn't talk much either, but when he did, if he didn't get the response he wanted, he'd take you apart, and he was just the fellow who could do it too, because he was one strong cook. He would say "I'm going to tell you something very interesting" and then go on and you'd better look interested; or "Let me tell you something very funny" and there had to be a lot of chortling and thigh-slapping after that.

None of the other ranch hands would play cards

with him any more because of that temper. We played cribbage, a game he taught me, and for two weeks running I lost my whole salary. Then I started figuring his game, and like all people who don't smile he had severe limitations. I started beating him with some regularity but he never paid, just kept score very neatly in a book he locked up in his locker every night, God knows why, but he locked everything up. He was scary. We had been playing two months or so when one night in his room, instead of getting his cards out of the locker, he took the book.

"Let me tell you something interesting."

"You bet, Smitty."

"I now owe you," and he read from the book, "a hundred and fifteen dollars."

"Say, that is interesting. A hundred and fifteen, eh?"

"Now I'll tell you something funny. I'm not going to pay you."

"Oh, that's a hoot. Not going to pay me."

"What I am going to do"—he was sharpening a butcher knife—"is I'm going to tell Mr. Kutcher that you have been doing a bang-up job and should be tried with the responsibility of ration buyer."

"I see." I didn't. Yet.

"For a month you'll buy the supplies. I'll tell my vendors to give you the same kickback deal I've had, and in that month you will get all I owe you and a little more."

"That's swell of you, Smitty."

"At the end of the month, you will quit. If you try to stay longer or get greedy and try to get more from our suppliers than I have, I shall have to . . ." and he ran the edge of that knife back and forth on one finger.

"Of course you will! And you'll be right to!"

Sure enough, exactly one month later, with some salary savings and about three bills that I'd been able to goniff from the ration allowance, I hightailed it for Los Angeles, California, with a ticket and seat and everything. Two weeks before I left, I wrote to my mom in Madison, Wisconsin to tell her where I was headed and there was a letter from her waiting for me at General Delivery in L.A. I have that letter to this day which I will now quote some passages from because it might help you as it has sure helped me.

Dear Son,
   What a delight to receive your oh so welcome letter! For you are ever present in my thoughts. After all, Tod, Jack is my firstborn, that's true and nothing can be done about that, but you are my baby, my perfected one. Please burn this letter, after you've read it, of course; I would not want it to fall into Jack's hands.
   I am so glad you left Rapid City and are striking out on your own. When you get to Los Angeles, call on Harry Tradler, the successful cousin of your dear late father's. Actually he is a second cousin but I am certain he will help you nevertheless.
   Things are well with Preston and me, as well as can be expected. Our spreading of the Pillar Of Fire movement here in Madison and its environs is going well e'en though the swimming is all upstream. Pres travels a lot and is doing well with the drug line especially with a cough medicine that he makes right here at home which has been a Godsend to your mother both as a boon to her health as well as the fact that since it is our own, the profit is a bundle, my dearest son. In fact with these same profits, Pres and I have bought into a neighborhood Eatery. We also sell a lot of cough medicine there.
   Since your father died I have had to be mom and dad both to you so I'll give some advice to you now even as d'Artagnan's father did 'or him because you are my own little musketeer, aren't you? Be true to your own self and then nobody can be untrue to you. Call things

by their right names and then you can deal with them. If you call a chair a chair, you can sit on it with perfect safety. If you call a picket fence a chair and sit on it, you could find certain parts of your body in agony. That's what men tell me and I have always believed men, that's been my G D problem.

But that is *my* problem and that's not what I'm writing about. In fact, if you want to do your dear mother a favor, it's don't worry about her. My cough is getting better. I just took another swig of your stepfather's cough medicine. It's a winner.

Let's see, what else? Oh, yes. Work hard and play hard. See the gravy of life, don't look underneath. Take caie of your body and it will take care of you. Make money and spend money; not all, because I know you will want to send some to your mother here in Madison, Wisconsin, not like your brother Jack, who doesn't even know who carried him till he weighed fourteen pounds or care. All right, I have forgotten that. I will of course save the money for you and that will get you on the right track of saving. That's what a mom is for.

Do all your own thinking, don't let anyone else do it for you. Our Pillar Of Fire movement teaches us never to join any group, a hard lesson to learn but worthwhile. For we are all identical at the source, just different in the expression of it. There is a universal Nature informing us all and we are each a personal prism through which that Nature expresses itself. Get the picture? Probably not, if I remember you right.

To go on. Stay out of groups! People are fine till they join together which is always to knock some poor soul on his head. I believe in personal vengeance because I can feel it, when someone hurts my baby, for instance, but I despise group vengeance. It is cowardly and untrue.

Am sending you some of this cough medicine and you must take it whenever you have a cough. Indeed, take it as I do, between coughs, to prevent same.

Do not compete with others, only with your own

potential. You can only be the best Toddy Fleedhurn possible. Compromise with others, but never with yourself, and above all, take your cough medicine always. You'll like it. It makes you feel popular.

Don't let anyone tell you what to do, not anybody. Certainly not your poor mother which you have never listened to her anyways.

Take care of yourself, my sweet son, and no matter how things go for you there in Los Angeles, remember that there is always a place for you. Not here, because we only have a small apartment, but God has a place for you somewhere.

Kindest personal regards,

Your adoring mother,
Mother

Those were words to live by then as they are now. I decided to call on my dear father's second cuz, Harry Tradler, but not until I had a stake and a wardrobe. I had about ninety dollars that I checked into the Hotel Cecil on Main Street with, got a meal at a classy restaurant called the Good Fellows' Grotto, and then went in search of and found a pool hall, which was called the Palace, where I ran my wad into $130 and met two swell hustlers named Dan and Rip who brought me to where they lived in a bungalow court in Hollywood named the Wisteria Villas and where I took an apartment the very next day for twenty-four dollars a month. They also showed me where I could buy some swag clothes and although I've never been one of those people who'd rather buy a hot suit for a double sawski than off the rack for eighteen fish, these looked like real value so I outfitted myself pretty good. I was ready to call Cousin Harry, who was, I was surprised to find out, known to my new pals and indeed one and all as the Shoe King of California.

Made an appointment with Harry Tradler's secretary to see him the following week. Since I figured he'd help me get a proper job, I went back to the Palace Pool Hall with Dan and Rip, where I ran my $130 into the ground, and then for the rest of the week we went to the beach in Rip's car. Rip was twenty-four, had been on the hustle about ten years, and Dan was about thirty-two and I had the feeling that he had once been legitimate, but of course I would never ask him. Anyway, he had a few dollars stashed somewhere and was always generous with us when we were in Tap City, as I certainly was now. Rip was always broke, I found out later, because whenever he did make a score, he blew it fast.

So this week we traveled on Danny, going to Muscle Beach every day to play volleyball, flirt with the girls, have hot dogs and beer, and talk. Until Monday came around, the day I had my 9:00 A.M. date with Harry Tradler. A big day for me I thought then and I think now.

His office was downtown, on Hill Street and 6th, if you know where that is. On the front of the building there was a big sign saying TRY A TRADLER and underneath "Tradler's Tuffees, Inc. 4th Floor." I go up, get directed to his secretary. She is a real sneaker, with the eyeglasses, a lot of black hair tied up, and she is so extra tall that the layman might miss the casabas, like misjudging a fat guy in a fight, how much muscle he can have underneath. What she was, she was long-legged and, like I say, a sneaker, so I know this is my man on the other side of the MR. H. TRADLER, Pres., PRIVATE door; I own him because I know who he is. Whatever it says on that door, he is a hustler, just like me. She shows me in, closes the door after me.

He is a medium-sized guy but he's got a big head. He's signing papers a mile a minute back there and without looking up he motions to a chair opposite him with his free hand.

"So you're Jack Fleedhurn's son, eh?"

"Yes, sir, that's about it."

"Always liked your father." He gets up and walks to the window. "Often wished I were more like him. Carefree, not torn apart by ambition like so many of us. But sweet. Never could figure out what Ellie saw in him. But she stuck with him. Though he never did accomplish much, did he?"

"Well, I like to think he raised a good son."

"You do have a brother, don't you? Anyway, I gather from your mother's letter that you are out here seeking your fortune. Or anybody else's, eh?"

"Ha ha. That's a good one, sir. But that is about the size of it."

"Funny thing your arriving today." Now he's looking out the window, his back to me. "Just this morning, I was thinking—I always think things out in the morning when the head is clear. I was thinking that after Edie and I had Nancy, she, Edith, that is, my wife, wanted another child and I always said, 'No, no, we have one perfect one. That's enough,' and she'd say, 'Don't you want a son?' 'Absolutely not,' I'd say, 'I do not want a son,'" and here he walks towards me and looks at me good. "But now I have changed my mind and I'm sorry. Maybe you could be the son I never wanted."

"I'd certainly like to try to be, sir." And I looked at him again, good. And I thought, This is the man I am going to be like. I thought of that brass plaque downstairs, and of the secretary with the sneaky knockers and of the way he had just sparred with me, testing and all, and I said to myself, "Follow that man, my boy, he knows where he's going and you sure as hell don't."

Harry went through the manual of arms with me, all the "Things are tough out here, but I'll try to do something" and "We must have lunch someday" and "Edith'll never forgive me if I don't have you out to the house for a home-cooked meal—of course she's taking her ceramic classes," finishing strong with "Leave your number with Miss Perez out front." But I knew I had him.

So for a week I worked for a guy named Curly Walker I had had the good fortune to meet at the Palace Pool Hall, handling the stick in a small crap game in Van Nuys at nights, and I went to the beach during the day. Then I hear from Miss Juanita Perez, who couldn't have been friendlier.

"Mr. Fleedhurn? This is Juanita Perez, Mr. Tradler's secretary."

"Oh, hi."

"How do you like our sunny Southern California clime?"

"It's swell, Miss Perez."

"Mr. Tradler would like you to go to the Mountain Moss Company, that's one of Tradler's Tuffees' biggest outlets, and report to Mr. Ralph Borelli. He's expecting you. I don't think I'm supposed to say anything, but I believe there's a job waiting for you there. Please don't say I said anything about that."

"Oh, no. And I do appreciate your telling me."

"I guess you know Mr. Tradler pretty well, don't you?"

"Well, our families are almost related. And I think they were in some business deals together."

"Is that so? Is there anything else I can do for you, Tod? You don't mind if I call you Tod, do you? You can call me Juanita."

"Thanks, Juanita."

"I don't live too far from you and I have a car, if you'd like to be shown around. I'd simply be more than happy to. And maybe you'd like a home-cooked Mexican meal. I get tired of cooking just for myself."

"How kind you are! How thoughtful! I will call on you to do just that as soon as I've cleared up this little ailment I have—well, you might say it's a disease—but as soon as the doctor gives me the O.K. to, I'll call you."

That was all I needed, to go foraging on my Chosen Mentor's Private Preserves.

Next day I went to Mountain Moss after the job. I had absolute certainty that my future lay with this man, Harry Tradler. And when I got to the retail outlet he had in Mountain Moss, with signs like TRADLER'S TUFFEES—YOUR FOOT WILL WEAR OUT FIRST OR MONEY CHEERFULLY REFUNDED and TRADLER'S TOE HUGGERS, I was feeling pretty good.

The Mountain Moss Company was the first big building in downtown Los Angeles: seven stories high and a block square. A department store founded by Col. Tom Mountain, who "almost rode with Teddy and the Rough Riders in '98" but had wound up as a big buyer for the Quartermaster Corps in Washington during W.W. I. And who sold him all the shoes for the brave doughboys? That's right, that favorite mentor of mine, star of "They Also Serve Who Sit and Sell Shoes," Harry Tradler, courtesy of his financial backer AND father-in-law Nathaniel J. Moss. Kickback is an ugly word, but now here was this store, one of a chain of six, with Col. Tom and Nat as partners, Harry T. as a major shareholder and custodian of all the shoe concessions. Friendships formed in trade never die. The friends have too much on each other.

Then who is Ralph Borelli, you are asking, the one

you're reporting to? He is the elevator starter in this place and I will be an elevator operator because I know Harry Tradler and there is a uniform that fits me. How come there is a job open, Fleedhurn? Because the way I've been able to fit this story together, Lieutenant, this Borelli, see, is a guy what takes himself seriously. And one of his operators was sitting in his car on the top floor idly having a sandwich with his door closed—this is the first elevator bank west of Chicago with elevator phones—and he answers with a mouthful of food and all that comes out is "Glub, Glub" while this idiot Borelli is trying to tell him to come down.

To make a short story, Colonel Tom Mountain happens to come around while Borelli is talking and inquires as to what is happening.

"It's Baumgarten, sir. He's on the top floor and I'm trying to talk him down."

"What's wrong with him, Borelli?" asks the good Colonel.

"Height rapture."

"Height rapture?"

"Yes, Colonel. I've seen it happen before. They don't want to come back down."

"Yes, I see. I've seen the same terrible thing happen to junior quartermaster officers with procurement slips. Good work. What's your name, young fellow?"

"Borelli, sir. Ralph Borelli."

So poor Baumgarten got himself made a floorwalker with strict instructions not to venture upstairs and Borelli was given a gold star or D.S.C. or something. But it never did him any good because although he took himself seriously, he did not take his job seriously (the opposite of the way it should be).

He wanted to be a baseball player. During the three years he had worked for the store and for fifteen years before that, he had gone to training camp and tried out for the Pittsburgh Pirates when they worked out in San Bernardino. Tried out every year, turned down every year. American stick-to-it-iveness loses again. He was crazed on the subject of baseball and would rather see Honus Wagner pick up a ground ball than Norma Talmadge do the kitchy-koo. He was a good-looking Italian guy, and I'd hear girls in the store invite him to dances and parties and all, and invariably he'd turn them down because he had to oil his glove or get his sleep and all that. Then, as I said, in March he'd leave the job, go to training camp, lose his seniority at the store, and then have to come back again.

That was my immediate superior. Get the picture?

I somehow managed to live through Borelli's daily inside jokes like "This job has its ups and downs" and slapped my thighs every time for the wit of them all and I drew my pay, which was twelve dollars a week, and of course I didn't let go my night job, although I could handle it only on Saturday nights, which were the best anyway, at Curly's crap game. I didn't hear again from Harry Tradler for about six weeks and I was beginning to wonder if I was following the right leader till one day they announced that the annual promotional tests were to be given that evening. I hadn't been there long enough to be eligible but Ralph Borelli had and he went up that night to take it. The test was overseen by a fellow I had got to know named Alistair Meadows and the reason I knew him was that he was one of those tiny geniuses who really could figure out anything but having no faith in themselves would then go against their figures. He was a regular tap-out at Curly's and was totally hung up on the gee-gees and all other gambling. You know the kind; they'll say, "There are only two horses in the race, Black Watch and Pretty Baby. According to my figures, Pretty Baby is a cinch. She will win the race." Then they bet on

Black Watch, Pretty Baby wins, and they say, "Didn't I tell you she was the best horse?" But they didn't bet on her. You've seen these people all over. Anyway, the way they gave the test was the applicant had three sets of questions with squares next to the question marked True or False, or Yes or No. So he would put an X in the square he thought was right, do as many as he could in the hour they gave him, and go home. Then the electric eye, which was a primitive clumsy affair in those days, would pick up the X if it was in the right box and grade accordingly. A perfect score was 200. The highest score ever recorded anywhere was 146. The Old Quartermaster, Col. Mountain, loved these tests. He thought it showed how little everybody else knew.

Now Ralph Borelli, either on his own or in his effort to be what he thought ball players were like, was a cluck. He had trouble reading Happy Hooligan and it was all he could do to put on his shin guards and cut off a chaw of tobacco without amputation.

You can guess what happened. The tests were fed into Col. Mountain's Great Machine, the Electric Eye looked at them and graded them and spat out the results into the Personnel Department, which Alistair took, brought down to the Colonel's office the next day, and then silently handed to the Old Man. One hundred and three employees had taken the exam, a grade of 90 made the applicant eligible for promotion, the highest grade anyone got was 122—except Ralph Borelli, who got 200. That's right, he scored Perfect. The Colonel, according to Alistair, looked at the perfect score, got all red, got all white, and then said hoarsely:

"I always believed if it ever happened, it would happen to my command."

"It's the training we all get here, sir," Alistair said.

"Thank you, Meadows."

Alistair had checked the test paper itself and found that Borelli had put an X in every box: Trues, Falses, Yesses, Noes. What did he care? What did he know? So the Electric Eye had picked up the correct answers and blurted out "Poifect." But Alistair hated the Colonel for being stupid and rich and had kept his mouth shut. The Old Man had promoted Borelli on the spot to be his Executive Aide. He asked Alistair to recommend someone for the starter's job. He put me up for it figuring, correctly, that I would give him a break Saturday nights making change at Curly's crap game, and the next thing you know I was sewing "Elevator Starter" on my uniform.

The next day I get another call from Miss Juanita Perez telling me that Mr. and Mrs. Harry Tradler would like me to come to lunch a week from the next Sunday at one o'clock at their home at 714 North Rodeo Drive in Beverly Hills. Success breeds success.

Dan and Rip drove me up to Beverly Hills early, about an hour before I was due at Tradler's, and we invested in one of those maps they push on tourists so that I would know just what I was getting into. Rod La Rocque lives here and Lon Chaney lives there and all that. We figured it was a good investment at fifty cents. Dan, who, as I told you, had once lived among real people and not only scufflers, said that no one ever arrived less than twenty-five minutes late and he recommended a half hour for me. But we had already driven past the house several times by 1:25 and I made them drop me off. It was an expensive house all right, but I had been getting psyched up for the battle like football players before the game and I wanted to get in there. They said they'd come back for me in four hours, and I figured I could stick it out that long.

I went up the flagstone walk to the door, which was mighty imposing, pulled the knocker which in turn rang a bell. The door was opened by a butler who was just pulling on the second sleeve of his white jacket. I got a flash of Tradler scurrying up the stairs in an undershirt while leaving one carpet slipper on the stone steps. The butler showed me into a room that was bigger than the whole bungalow-court apartment

Dan, Rip, and I lived in, all three of us. He murmured, "Martini?" and I noded curtly, and while he was handing me this cocktail glass, in walked the most beautiful lady I ever saw in my whole life.

When I was about twelve or thirteen, I used to read *Snappy Stories*, a magazine popular around the Dakotas. The description of the heroine usually went like "Sandra had long, red hair and green, slanted eyes. If she had a flaw, perhaps the mouth was too generous for the uptilted nose. And maybe her breasts were too firmly placed high above the slender waist," etc., etc., and I would think, It's not a flaw, I'll take it, I'll take it. Well, this lady was gorgeous. Her knockers were fighting like tigers to get out of the dress. And her lips were too wet. Some flaw. I was eating a peanut—they had everything around there—so my mouth was full when she introduced herself.

"Hi, you must be Tom. Harry's told me so much about you. I'm Edie Tradler." She gave me her hand in a cool grip. Fifty years ago and I can still feel it. And see those wet lips. "Has Carruthers taken good care of you?"

"Just phlub." A piece of the goober flew and whether it went on her face or not I don't know and I don't want to know.

"Well, I'm not going to let a guestie drink alone, especially a new guestie," and she poured some Martini from the oversized container into a glass. Not into a cocktail glass like mine but into a nice-sized water tumbler. Get the picture?

"Oh! Would you believe Miss Forgetful? I was so excited about meeting you—" she sloshes down about half her drink—"Harry told me so much about you and all, that I forgot this wasn't my papaya juice and I poured it into the wrong glass. I always open up the day with my papaya juice—"another swig—"it's got so many vitamins. Shall we go into the pool area?" We stepped out of the house into the bright sunlight.

"Holy Christ!" She put one hand over her eyes while she squinted and loped over to a round metal table that had a big beach umbrella over it and some chairs around, while I followed. "I forgot about the goddam sun."

Then followed the most wonderful twenty minutes of my life. It's funny, if you asked me the next day or week, I couldn't have told you anything that happened but now I remember every moment of it. That's the way my life was then: the minutes seemed like eternities and the years flew by. All very painful and I guess necessary, but never again. I mean if Mephisto popped into my office right now and said "Give me your soul and you can be nineteen again" I'd tell him to shove that deal right up his ass. And I don't even like my soul.

Yes, we had these few moments alone before the other guests arrived; the only interruptions we had were when Carruthers came out to refill my cocktail glass and her tumbler, which she forgot to change because she was so engrossed with what she was telling me. The gist of it all was that although she had a beautiful home that cost $110,000 new and was worth a whole lot more now, approximately double, and a husband she loved and respected, and I figured she really did because her eyes teared up every time she mentioned him, and a healthy daughter and a lot of friends, as I would see shortly, she said, still she was a very lonely woman.

Look, I had never heard a pitch like that before and I fell hard. It never occurred to me that you could have all the extra added attractions and not the feature. I was in ell oh vee ee, and that was that, no explanation.

Though I was almost twenty years old and had been

around a little, I was behaving like a kid with her, with Edie. Let's face it, nobody falls like a smart guy, win or lose.

I'm nineteen again, I feel like nineteen again, that nineteen-year-old boy lives in me and I owe him, I don't know what I owe him, but I'm always trying to pay him, to please him. And once in a while I do, goddammit. Can you imagine what that party meant to me, with the life I had led? All those beautiful people, that home, the swimming pool, the whole mosaic made complete by Edith's knockers.

All the guests seemed to arrive at once. Mr. Tradler ("Call me Harry," he said, "on Sundays") came out wearing cream-colored silk trousers and a wild, flowered Hawaiian sport shirt. I resolved to get one of those shirts the next day; I worshipped that man, he was God to me. In fact as the day went on I got to feeling smaller and smaller and more grateful: around him and all those beautiful people. The first to arrive after me was a man, oh I guessed he was about thirty-five, sandy hair, skin bronzed, eyes blue, blue sport shirt, and scarlet silk scarf.

It's like yesterday, it's just like yesterday, and I'm grateful again. His name is Chuck Robbins, he's Harry's assistant, and he has a girl with him who's wearing—Leroy, bring me a glass of ice water—a brassiere which they call a halter and long wide flowing trousers very tight around the seat. Long hair, sweet-looking casabas, and high, high heels. Her name is Babs and I remember looking at her and thinking, I'm certainly glad I am in love with Edie because otherwise . . .

Within a half hour thirty more guests arrived and they were all beautiful—I mean well groomed, gleaming clean and manicured, everyone's clothes looking new. The kind of people that always make me feel like my nose is running. They looked rich and some of them were. A few changed into bathing suits and went into the pool. Harry offered me a suit but I didn't go in because my arms were skinny and I was white all over, chalk white. And miserable because I didn't feel I fit in, in fact knew I didn't. After about an hour, who do you think came in?

Jack Holt. Jack Holt, the movie star actor. And a sweeter guy you'll never find. Harry introduced us and Jack gripped my hand, looked me straight in the eye, and said "Hello." Is that a wonderful human being? I mean, he was a star and could have said *anything* to me, if you know what I mean. Since that time I have bought and sold dozens of movie stars but you never get over being in love with the first one. The late great Jack Holt.

That's the way it all went for a couple of hours, people drinking and swimming and me with a half smile listening a lot and nodding while watching Harry. Every now and then Edie would walk by and whisper "Try to have a good time" and squeeze my hand. At one point while Harry was at the barbecue with a big white hat on and an apron that said "Sure I can cook" except there was a huge orb in place of the "I," I was in a group listening to him tell how he founded his empire. In the group were Chuck Robbins and the lady with the long hair, who was, I'd found out, his wife.

"How did you get started, Harry?" one of the men asked, a leather salesman from Detroit.

"Just luck, I guess," Harry said. "And keeping plenty of nine-and-a-half Charlies in stock." That's the most popular shoe size.

"Luck, he says." The leather salesman laughed while he looked at me. That was the first time he ever looked at me including when we were introduced.

"Yes, luck," Harry went on. "Let's face it, I was simply born with the ability to work a little harder than the next guy."

"I see." The leather salesman looked at Harry with concentration. "I see."

"And I was fortunate enough to have the foresight to see that if a man, let's say, for the sake of argument, a man with intelligence, drive, and stick-to-it-iveness, a man who could and would manufacture shoes *and* maintain a chain of clean shoe stores within which to market said shoes, a man who knew his business and didn't overpay his help and had the guts not to listen to a bunch of wise little acres who told him it couldn't be done" (I noticed Harry was glaring at a little old man with gray hair standing by the pool who I found out later was Edie's father. The old guy wasn't listening to Harry; in fact he had just pinched the thigh of a very pretty girl who then leaned down and kissed him on the nose. He pinched her again), "why then, that individual could become a millionaire." Harry raised his voice. "A millionaire many times over."

"But how did you actually get started, Harry?" a lady asked while Harry thoughtfully regarded a hamburger that he took off the fire, burnt to a crisp. He put it on a bun, looked at it again, and passed it on to me.

"How did I get started?" Harry considered the question, then glared at her while he removed another hamburger, also charred down to the size of a half dollar.

"I'll tell you how I got started. I started as an eleven-dollar-a-week clerk working in a store in Sedalia, Missouri. Sedalia, Missouri, mind you, no advantages there like certain other persons I could name—and I stayed there for two and a half years, learning my trade, that of shoe clerk, you see. Then with a borrowed $50,000 I opened my first factory."

"And the rest is history," breathed the leather man.

"But then, like I said, I've been lucky and a good merchant."

"And a liar," Chuck Robbins said quietly. You could have heard a shoelace drop.

"I beg your pardon?"

"Chuck, please." His wife was plucking at his silk sleeve.

"I said a liar." Chuck shook her hand off his arm. "Leave me alone, honey. Maybe I've had enough to drink to tell what I really feel. I say you're a liar, Harry. Because you just said you're a good merchant. You're not a good merchant." He took a swig from his frosty glass, weaving a little. "You're a *great* merchant."

"Well, I wouldn't know about that, Chuck."

"Well I would!"

"You don't have to get belligerent about it." Harry laughed.

"I'm not getting belligerent. It's just that everyone thinks you're perfect, but you've got a flaw. Eff ell ay double-you."

"Puh-leeze, Chuck," said his wife again, same sleeve plucking, same wife.

"You sell yourself too short. That's your flaw, Harry Tradler."

"Please, Chuck, leave Harry alone and eat your sandwich."

"No," said Harry. "Chuck is speaking his mind and I respect that. We can all use a little honest criticism, if we're man enough to take it. And I hope I'm that." He lifted his head, looked Chuck squarely in the eye, and extended his hand, which Chuck shook. I knew I might never see anything like that again.

And so it went. Everybody was drinking pretty good including the undersigned and there suddenly appeared a three-piece Hawaiian band so there was dancing and swimming and throwing of persons into the pool and just gay, gay, gay. Meantime I was sweating like a steer from the bootlegged booze and the heat and my jacket which I couldn't take off because of the short-sleeved shirt and skinny arms underneath. But I'd found a bathroom with boxes of Kleenex so I kept the tissues strapped under my arms with adhesive tape from the medicine cabinet, thereby cutting down on the dark stains at the jacket armpits. About six o'clock I got up to leave but Edie saw me and said, "Stick around, please. Let some of the others leave but we'll just be family for supper." So I sat down again.

Of course no one left at all, except Jack Holt. And this time Carruthers and a big Swedish lady showed up to make steaks and corn and salad. I didn't know what to do about Rip and Dan in the car outside, but what the hell, this was the Main Chance and I knew they'd understand.

Then it was deep dark and suddenly I'm in the corner of the garden trying to sop up the alcohol with hamburger and corn and fresh strawberries smothered in heavy cream when I hear a sniffling sound. I turn around and there on the grass is Edie fighting back the tears. Well, you know the stories you hear when you're a kid—"Always bang nurses, they know how to take care of theirself," and that stuff. This time I remembered something Little Jack told me before he went overseas. "Two times you can be sure of getting laid is when the dame is drunk or crying." I went over and sat next to her.

"What's the matter, Edith?"

"What's the matter?" Sniffle, sniffle, then the bitterest laugh I'd ever heard. "My friend, my best friend, Bitsy Whitehorse over there" and she pointed her glass across the pool to a lady with long dark hair who was dancing with a young man who was wearing a red shirt tied at the waist. Bitsy threw her head back and laughed real loud while he threw her into some kind of mad fandango. "Her brother-in-law's nephew, Howie, has conjunctivitis of the eye. God, when will it all stop?" And she emptied her glass. I couldn't blame her.

"But are you O.K.,Edie?"

"Oh, I'm O.K." She started to get up but fell back. "Someone has to stay O.K. I'm just curious, that's all, just curious. I want to know why me? Why does everything always happen to me?"

I put my arm around her and she fit swell.

"I get up in the morning and try to meet each day with everything I've got and then, Wham! I mean, that boy is sixteen and could lose the sight of his whole eye." She grabbed my thigh in what is known as a viselike grip and I almost fainted. "Do you have any idea what that means, Tod? Do you have any idea? A teen-aged Cyclops. An object of scorn to all and he won't even be able to see who is scorning him." Then she simply sat still in my arms and sipped from her drink. No more tears, no complaining, just a brave little Edith living with her grief. She was Miss Guts to me.

"You see—how old are you, Toddy?"

"I'm almost twenty."

"Twenty. Well, you may not understand this yet."

"Of course."

"I love my husband. I make a nice home for him." She waved her arm around, splashing me a bit. "Because he has suffered. All those years in Sedalia, Missouri, working around feet. It does something to a man, they can go crazy. Then we met, we married, and my father put him in business."

"Was that old guy doing the tango your father?"

"Yes. He made Harry president of the company, but what Harry never figured on was having to work. Daddy kept controlling interest in the stock and every year at the stockholders' meeting he calls for a vote to throw Harry out of the job. Then he votes to retain him for one more year but Harry lives on the crest of that volcano and it's all my fault. What's your home phone number?"

"Ivar 4166. You mustn't blame yourself, Edie dear."

"Why not? Everyone else blames me." She got up suddenly, pushing my hand aside. "Even you blame me." She walked away, in the direction of the bar.

When I saw her again a few minutes later she had her arm through Harry's listening to him tell another crowd what a wonderful guy he was. Well, he was, he was. She didn't even notice me when I went over to say good-bye and thank you. Harry gave me a smile and a handshake with his left hand and went on talking away.

It was a little after nine when I got to the car. Rip and Dan were asleep in it. I felt guilty, hanging them up all that time, but they were great about it.

"How was the party, great?" Rip asked eagerly.

"Just couldn't have been better. Lots of food, plenty to drink, and they even had a band, a three-piece band."

"Did you drink too much?" asked Dan. "You didn't get out of line, did you?"

"Oh no, Dan."

"Who all was there?" said Rip. "I'll bet there was somebody famous there, there must have been."

"Jack Holt, that's who was there."

"Jack Holt! Hey, you're running in class, kid."

"It can't hurt you to be seen at a party with Jack Holt," said Dan thoughtfully.

"What about quiff? We saw some knockouts going in before we went to sleep," said Rip.

"Oh, sure. But nothing special," I lied. I couldn't tell them anything about Edie. That was sacred.

I sent up those elevators about 84,000 times during the next week and a half and in the lunch breaks sat around the Thrifty Drug Store listening to the other proles expressing their hate for The Store and for the customers who hated The Store. The slaves wanted to keep the system just in case one of them got to the top in time to kick somebody in the teeth. Rebels don't want to tear down the castle, they want to live in it, right? Well, they're living in it now, with their damn unions. Let's see how well they do, let's see if they can make 84,000,000 bucks!

Ten days after the party, I heard from Edith.

By this time I had what they call a single at Wisteria Villas, where Rip and Dan had a double. Mine had a Murphy bed in the wall and a kitchenette. Rip and Dan had a phone in theirs and that was the number I had given Edith, get the picture? I was sitting with the boys playing hearts at a nickel a point when the phone rang. Rip answered and said, "For you. A lady and I think she's crying. Do you know anyone who's crying?"

"Toddy, is that you? I'm supposed to be at the movies with Bitsy, but I suddenly thought why don't I have another nice talk with Toddy Fleedhurn instead. I suppose you're busy, though."

"No, no, not at all."

"Then can I see you?"

"Sure. Where?"

"How about your place. Can we be alone there?"

The rest would soon be history. I went back to my bungalow to wait for her and she soon showed up toting a fifth of Seagram's Best Canadian Whiskey, a "house gift." The least I could do was open it and pour us a couple of drinks and the most she could do was to tell me what a brave little person she was before I had one hand down her dress on a nervy little nipple and she was grabbing my joint which was eminently grabbable at the time. We got the Murphy bed down from the wall with a crash and hurled ourselves in it, tearing off clothes on the way. Then we went at it like knives and forks.

"Kiss it, kiss it here. Kiss it there. Kiss this. Let me kiss you. BITE IT! Put your finger there. Oh my God! Oh baby!"

I thrust my cock into her and we went crazy up and down, sideways, every which way and then we came together, and when we did, that whole bed started to shake from its wall springs, the whole room seemed to move, the lights went out and on again, the picture fell off the wall.

I rolled over, and Edith couldn't take her eyes off me, and for once there was no glassiness in them. She looked at me like I was God or someone.

What we did not know, what I found out in the papers the next morning but what she never knew because she woke up too late to read them, was that at that very moment there had been a nice little Southern California earthquake. Just a small tremor but enough to make all the popular seismographs, two columns in the Eastern newspapers, and Edith Tradler think I was the great lover of her life.

From then on she manipulated her free time to come by Wisteria Villas every late afternoon when I got home from work and even drop off little presents for me with the boys like silk dressing gowns, cologne, and home-baked chocolate brownies, hundreds of them. I mean, she wanted to cook for me, sew for me, the whole lot. She even took to hanging around the Mountain Moss Company so she could ride up and down in the elevator with me.

On the weekends, while Harry was in town, I was at the house, swimming in the pool and in general being the son that Harry never wanted and the lover that Edie always wanted. The tail was great and the presents never stopped, to say nothing of the pineapple upside-down cake and the corn bread and everything else. But I was getting to feel like a prisoner. People wanted me to belong to something again and I still didn't want to. Harry would talk to me about Freemasonry, and most of all about the Fellowship of Business and where my place would be in it if I really applied myself and stuck to the rules.

And Edith wanted to mold me too. It's like I was wearing a blue double-breasted suit and she was saying, "That's the most gorgeous suit I have ever seen. I want one just like it. Except that I want mine to be brown and plaid and single-breasted." Edith would breathe into my ear "I'm crazy about your hair, your eyes" and then she would send me to another barber and she even tried to pluck my eyebrows.

She also wanted me to follow a certain line of talk, to talk about myself, what the kids today call "getting into your head." God knows she talked about herself enough, and that's how all the trouble started.

She came over to Wisteria Villas one night with a tureen of spaghetti sauce when Harry was addressing a calf tanners' convention at the Biltmore Hotel. After the festivities in the Murphy bed, while she was cooking up the spaghetti and drinking the red wine she kept at my place, she started talking about her marriage. And I hated that. It made me feel scared. I wonder now, a half-century later, how many times I've been on the other side of that conversation.

"I can't complain," she began, stirring with one hand, drinking with the other. Woman's work is never done. "It's just that Harry wants so much to look good. We have to live our life like in a photograph album."

She splashed out the pasta and sauce and we carried it to the little table. She was more thoughtful than I'd ever seen her but not too much so to let go the wine. I just hoped she wasn't going to start crying again.

"Sometimes we get all dressed to go downtown and I know Harry is preparing for another picture in our album." By now she was spitting the words out, also some of the spaghetti. "'Here are Edie and Harry at the opera.' Look" and she laughed, "he's even wearing an opera cape!"

She came around the table and sat on my lap, all the while balancing her cigarette and the big water tumbler of wine, like that vaudeville act with the plates spinning on poles. "You don't know how hard it is, keeping up a cheerful look for him while he plays that photograph-album game. You've seen it. 'Here are Edith and Harry at the barbecue'" and she flashed a horrible fake smile at me, "and look, here's Harry and Edie at the Red Cross Drive Headquarters and here's Harry and Edie here and there and here's Harry and Edie having a serious heart-to-heart talk and here's Edie cheating with her husband's protégé and here's Edie telling Harry all about it."

I stood up, dumping her and the food and the wine all over.

"What the hell are you talking about?"

"Oh, I know it's going to happen," she sniffled from the floor, "and it's all your fault."

"Don't blame me, I'm just an innocent bystander!" I had a feeling between the shoulder blades, as if a knife had its point there.

"There's no such thing!" she yelled. "All bystanders are guilty. And you're the guiltiest of the whole bunch. Oh Tod," she sobbed from the floor, "I love you so much how can you do this to me?"

And of course I did. Did you ever run down a lot of stairs, picking up speed as you ran, knowing the whole time that you were going to miss a step and fall on your face, get your nose bloody, knock all your teeth out, lose consciousness, and then of course it happens? That was what my life was like the next few weeks. Edith kept coming over and we kept pulling the Murphy down and getting at it like mad while she'd breathe, "Make it like the first time, baby, make it like the first time." Why didn't I ever tell her about that earthquake? Pride? But what the hell, if I had, maybe I wouldn't be here today, a millionaire many times over.

Through this whole period I seemed to be holding my breath. I was waiting for Harry to find out, the way a gambler hangs around the table waiting for that seven that'll clean him out, an alcoholic waits for that last drink that will black him out. When I was at the Tradler house I could hardly talk to anyone, and I couldn't even confide in Rip or Dan, all of which made me so lonely I wanted to weep at times. I remember, during that period, I was taking the trolley downtown and it was awfully crowded. I paid my fare to the conductor, who said, "Step in the back of the trolley" and I thought, Why doesn't he want me to stay here with him? Doesn't he like me any more? What did I do wrong? Why can't we sit down and talk this thing out like two grown people? I was just taking life personally and it was agony. Then the axe really did fall. I got word on the elevator that Mr. Tradler wanted me to come to his office after work. I thought, What the hell. It's only thirty blocks away. It's the least I can do for the guy.

I swear that's all I thought. That and what do the words "scared shitless" mean to you as a person?

I got to Harry's in about thirty-four minutes, which
was as long as I could take going as fast as I could. I
thought I saw anger on Juanita Perez's lovely greasy
face but I was reading everything from myself, so I
don't know if it really was there. She took me in to
Harry almost immediately. He was signing things as
usual but stopped long enough to wave to me to sit
down. When I looked around the office this time, I
noticed things I didn't remember ever having seen. A
framed document on the wall that proclaimed Harry
Tradler a member of the official Union Pacific 100,000
Mile Club. His high-school diploma. A plaque pro-
claiming Harry the recipient of the Splendid American
Award for 1919 given by The Brothers of Nathan Hale.
A picture of Harry and his father-in-law, with the old
man wearing a beatific smile. A fuzzy picture of Jack
Holt autographed to Harry in white ink. A shot of
Harry in a funny paper hat and tuxedo, an arm around
Edie, who is cutting a cake that has on it "Happy
Tenth Anniversary" and looking worshipfully up at
Harry. On the desk, facing me where I sat, also framed
but on its stand, in Gothic print, "When the going gets
tough, the tough get going." That's exactly what I

wanted to do: get going. Then Harry looked up, smiling.

"Let's sit over here." He led me to the leather couch, where we sat next to each other. He twisted around so that we were facing each other. He was still smiling, but for the first time I noticed how big he was: the powerful hands and chest.

"Comfy?" he asked and I nodded, hoping my head would come off and the interview would be over.

"Want a nice cold drink?"

I nodded. He unlocked his closet that had the bar in it and came back with two drinks.

"Here's mud," he said, touching my glass with his and drinking up. I took a swallow of mine and kept staring at him like a cobra at a mongoose. A very powerful mongoose. He sat down next to me again.

"There is some talk around that you have been fucking my wife."

I took another large swallow but not of the drink.

"Now where would you hear an awful thing like that?"

"From my wife."

"From Edith?"

"Drink up," he said. I did. The drink smelled like bitter almonds, an odor in the murder novel I was reading. "What's the matter, kid? Your drink all right? Good. Now listen, kid, we're both men of the world, right? I understand these things." I remember noticing everything now, a mark on the table, a spot on the rug.

"*Actually when the shot was fired, deponent was two and a half feet from the wall and the victim slid directly on the floor where a pool of blood ensued,*" I could almost hear myself saying.

"*Two and a half feet? How did you know that?*" *snaps the district attorney.*

"I measured it, that's why, because I measured it. See?"

"No further questions." The DA bites his mustache, defeated. I sit calmly.

". . . and let's face it, I know my Edie. So there's no sense making a federal case of it."

"That's mighty . . ."

"I would advise you not to talk, kid. And I'd like to give you a little more advice, if you don't mind?"

"Anything."

"I think you should go out of town for a little while."

"Oh, yes. For how long, do you think, Harry?" I was beginning to feel comfortable again.

"For the rest of your life." He handed me his breast-pocket handkerchief to wipe up the drink I spilled on my jacket.

"I thought you said 'a little while.'"

"If you don't go out of town, the rest of your life will only be a little while."

"Oh."

"It's what we in the shoe game call a paradox."

"Well, thanks a lot for calling that to my attention. I appreciate it."

"Not at all. I was a good friend of your father's."

"He can't run you out of town," said Rip when we had a high-level conference that night, he and Dan and I, about my predicament. "This is a free country. Our guys didn't slog through the mud of France so that one man in a seat of power can put his Tradler Tuffee on the neck of a lonely boy. What can he do to you?"

"He can hire a half-dozen bruisers to come over here," said Dan, "and beat the shit out of Tod *and* his friends. There could be six broken legs at Wisteria Villas."

"On the other hand," said Rip, "what are we fighting for? An elevator starter's job? Is the game worth the candle?"

"I think you should get out of town, kid," said Dan.

"Where in the world can I go? I sure as hell am not going back to South Dakota."

"Why don't you ship out to sea?" Dan suggested. "I saw you reading that book by Conrad last Sunday, so you must have a feeling for it."

"That's right." Rip was getting enthused. "Why don't you join the navy? Learn a trade. Get a girl in every port. That's a good trade."

"He doesn't have to join the navy. Go down to Long Beach; there are ships leaving every day for the Orient, South America. I did it when I was your age."

"And look at that man today." Rip was on a pitch. "You've got to do it, Toddy. The wind in your hair, stars for a blanket, a good teak deck 'neath your feet. What more could a man want?"

"I'll do anything you fellows say." As I said this who walked in the door but Edith.

"Hi, Rip. Hi, Danny." She was bright-eyed and beautiful today, no sign of tears. Gave me a kiss on the ear and sat down, handing a paper bag with a bottle in it to Danny. "Here's a housewarming present, direct from and gift wrapped by your neighborhood family bootlegger."

"Why, thanks."

"Will you have one with us?" said Rip.

"I thought you'd never ask."

So Dan gave her a drink and then the rest of us and we talked small talk till it almost broke our backs. Edie was dying for them to go back to their own apartment so she could get her ashes hauled and I wanted them to stay there so I wouldn't get my legs broken by an irate hubby-wubby. I was trying to get them to stay, but she kept saying things like "You two must be busy" and "Don't let us keep you." However, as you know, when a man and a woman get on the field of battle, the man must lose because really strong men simply don't get into jousting matches with ladies. So the boys went back to their apartment after a half hour or so and there I was with my beautiful doom.

"Harry told me that you and he had a little talk."

"Edie," I said, "why did you do it? Why did you have to tell him about us?"

"Because I didn't want us to have anything sordid in our lives. What we have had is too beautiful, too fine ever to be spoiled by lies, lies, lies. Do you think I would do anything to hurt you?"

"I love you too, Edith. Even though you do have a big mouth."

"But it's a pretty mouth, isn't it?" and she leaned forward with the juicy wetness of it which I kissed.

"Edith, this can't go on. It's not fair to you, it's not fair to Harry, who has, let's face it, been mighty good to me, and it's not fair to me—I could be killed. I'm leaving town tomorrow."

"Then let's have one for the road."

I know it sounds romantic, but that was the best bang we ever had, the best one for me, that is. For her I guess the first one, when I was aided and abetted by Mother Nature, will always be the best. "Shattering" was the word she usually used to describe it.

The next day, as good as my word, I took off—for San Francisco.

I went to San Francisco which I decided was a more romantic place to sail from and besides if Harry should suddenly decide to put lighted sticks under Rip's and Dan's fingernails, all they could tell him would be "Long Beach." I was grateful I had gotten out whole because Harry had been planning to guide me up the ladder of success till I would die of exhaustion, as his father-in-law was doing to him. And Edie piling into that apartment every chance she got with presents until I had practically no manhood left. I had learned things and I was alive. Perfect. But then I always have been able to see the half-full bottle instead of the half-empty and I truly believe that's why I'm such a smash hit today and loaded beyond dreams of avarice. Why, if I fell out of a twenty-story window, all the way down I'd be thinking "What a swell chance to learn how to land properly." And as I bounced up again I'd be figuring how to sell tickets for the next jump.

I went down to the docks every day, and as I saw those great ships my heart was filling more with the desire, the need, to go to sea. The spray in the hair, the hair in the eyes, the eyes looking ahead to the ever-appearing horizon. It all beat the hell out of the six ball in the side pocket. I had plenty of loot in my kick because Edith didn't let me go off short and I found myself buying drinks for an old salt who fed my dream.

"Aye, lad, when you're up there in the crow's-nest alookin' at the stars, you get closer to nature, to God, and, yes, to yerself."

"Isn't it cold up there?"

"Of course it is! But yer warm inside because then ye are yer own man and canna belong to any man. I'll have another beer."

"Sure. I'll bet you've seen a lot, haven't you."

"Seen a lot. Ha! Have ye ever seen a fish as big as a building? The whale, the whale. Watch out for him."

"Well, I believe the whale, technically, is not a fish but is more your mammal. Isn't that right?"

"I'll have another beer."

"I'll bet when I stand a night watch alone, like you said, I'll finally get closer to my real self."

"That's right, though why you'd want to I'll never know."

For ten days that whole thought of the wind, the rain, the sun, the sky, the man's work, and all that obsessed me as I kept applying for jobs.

I shipped out on the *Empress of Japan*, bound for Honolulu and Kobe, as an elevator operator. This was the first vessel on the Pacific Coast sporting one of these and of course I was the only man on the docks with the proper experience.

As the ship pitched forwards and backwards twenty-four hours a day, I went up and down fourteen hours a day (sometimes I do feel the need for unions) and it was all uneventful until one dark night that changed my life. But not as much as it changed Mister Yamanamo's.

He was a short dark Japanese banker on A deck. I never saw him smile or heard him speak the three whole weeks he was aboard. "Red" Sutton, another passenger, an American, always smiled and greeted me when he got into my elevator on the way to and from the sun deck, where his cabin was. And when he got in at night after having had a good dinner and a few drinks, he'd tip me a dollar, good money in those days. He was such a friendly fellow, the kind we all like. I noticed too that after a week out he had somehow struck up an acquaintanceship with Mister Yamanamo. Sometimes they even rode up to the sun deck together.

But two nights before we were due to arrive at Honolulu I couldn't sleep and was lolling around the stern of the ship in the pitch black. There were no stars or moon out. I heard some low talk and suddenly a grunt. My eyes had got used to the dark by then and I could make out a form—Sutton's. I saw him lift something over his head and throw it into the drink.

Now when you consider that I am so suspicious by nature that I think every five-year-old is a midget hoodlum in disguise till proven otherwise, you can understand how I tried to shrink into the darkness, behind a winch. But I tripped on a rope, fell to the deck resoundingly, and Red came over and found me. I heard him coming and pretended to be asleep.

"Hello, kid. What're you doing here? Don't they give you a room?"

"Oh. Mr. Sutton. Oh. Well, I come out here some nights. Just to get close to the stars."

"Not many stars out tonight, kid." He offered me a cigarette which I assumed was poisoned and took immediately.

"I guess that's why I fell asleep."

"Well, you'll freeze your ass out here now. Come to my cabin and I'll get you a drink. Just to help you keep body and soul together."

Sounded like a good idea to me, especially since he had a grip on my arm like a boa constrictor. Down in his cabin he gave me a large glass of good whiskey with ice and everything, fixed it all himself, made me sit in the best chair, then he sat on the bunk, slapped his hands on his knees, looking pleased as a Derby winner.

"Guess you saw me on deck, throwing that bundle overboard."

I was about to tell him that I'd been asleep when suddenly I remembered my father's words: "A lie is the wust thing they is."

"Well, actually, now that you mention it, why, yes I did."

"What'd you think that bundle was, son?"

"Oh, your laundry, I guess. And I don't blame you a bit, Mr. Sutton. I know how bad the laundry service is here on board, and it doesn't pay to send it out so near Honolulu and all."

"You're not totally wrong, Tod. It is Tod, isn't it?"

I nodded feverishly.

"It was laundry, but it wasn't mine and there was someone in it. Mr. Yamanamo, to be precise."

"Precise . . ."

"Did you hear him say anything?"

"Say anything?"

"That's right." And for some reason, he slapped his knee, laughed, shook his head, and came over to me, but all he did was take away my glass to refill it.

"Well, I thought I heard someone say 'Help,' but it must have been the waves because I don't suppose it could have been Mr. Yamanamo since he didn't speak any English. So I really didn't hear anything except those waves, just those waves."

"Ever hear him talk at all?"

"No," I said. "Come to think of it, I never did."

"He spoke English better than you do." He smiled

again. "Not that that's so hard. Now, Tod, think about what you heard him say."

"I told you, Mr. Sutton. It sounded like 'Help!'"

"That's what it was. But only partly." He leaned forward again. "He said, 'Help me!'" He leaned back, his eyes never leaving my face. "And I did."

"I'm sure you did, Mr. Sutton."

Then he told me how Mr. Yamanamo had been a banker in Tokyo who had gone to New York on business. And while there met a blonde he got crazy about and she had pointed out a gambling hell on West 77th Street where he had dropped exactly $1,000,000 and had paid right up like a good soldier. And how it wasn't exactly his own money he had used but the Tokyo bank's. The managers of this particular gambling establishment were pals of "Red" Sutton's and so they had asked him to get on the same ship as Mr. Yamanamo and sort of look after him, to see that he didn't do anything foolish when he got back to Japan. Mr. Sutton didn't say what it might be, but I assume they didn't want the tiny banker to blow the whistle on the whole deal because then the authorities might have found out that all the people in the club, the players as well as the croupiers, were employees of the same management.

According to Mr. Sutton, and I was not prepared to doubt him at the time, Mr. Yamanamo was horribly embarrassed, knew he should commit hara-kiri to save his family's honor, and on deck that night was simply discussing the problem with Mr. Sutton, *i.e.*, that he didn't have enough nerve to go through with it.

As Mr. Sutton felt he should render assistance to his fellow man, he had tossed him overboard.

"That's why he was saying 'Help me,'" said Red. "It was really quite piteous."

"You certainly did help him, sir."

"Not for nothing do they call me 'The Helper.'"

The next day, we docked at Honolulu, and since Mr. Yamanamo's steward had reported his disappearance to the Captain, there was some questioning from the Hawaiian immigration authorities who knew that he was an important banker and of course they assumed he had somehow jumped ship for reasons of his own. They even got around to interrogating me.

"When did you see him yesterday afternoon?"

"When I took him upstairs, sir, in my own elevator."

"Did you see him again? After that?"

"When I took him downstairs, that was later on."

"Was that the last time you saw him?"

"No, I took him upstairs again, sir."

And so that went. I never lied to them, but I didn't volunteer anything either. I wanted to play ball with Mr. Sutton, who I felt had shown candor in all that he had told me and who, when we were discussing in his stateroom what I would say, was cleaning the biggest revolver I ever saw.

When we finally got to Kobe, I found that Mr. Sutton had cabled ahead for another ship to go on for us; he had also thoughtfully made arrangements with the Head Steward for me to leave my job. He was one of those men who do things easily, or seem to, like Joe DiMaggio or Gary Cooper. He never seemed to be thinking about or doing anything or planning anything. But take it from me, he was organized. The fact is that the two of us never got off a ship for more than a few hours before we went on another one until we got through the Suez Canal and we stopped in Egypt for a few days at Shepheard's Hotel.

During the whole trip, he never talked about himself. I still don't know where he came from, though he had been almost everywhere. He read a lot, adventure and history mostly, and he got me on to his favorite writers, which didn't do me any harm. Mark Twain, Herman Melville. He thought *The Confidence Man* by Melville was the best book he ever read.

We waited at Shepheard's for three or four days until Mr. Sutton got the cablegram he was waiting for. He read it while we were having a tall cool drink.

"Made a good score here once," he said as he folded and put the cable in his pocket. "And got this for it." He pulled down his collar a bit and indicated a scar on his neck.

"Gee, that's pretty close to the jugular. How did you get that?"

"An irate husband." He got up and put on his jacket. "Though he wasn't so irate till he lost his money."

We left the day he got the cable, by ship to Marseilles and from there we took the train to Paris.

Red checked us into the Hotel George V, and the first night, I thought we were just going out to dinner, he took me to a club called Joe Zelli's. The jazz band there saw Red enter, stopped what it was playing, and swung into "Sing Hallelujah." He was some apple. He walked right over to a table and introduced me to two men, and my life took another turn for the next dozen years.

The first man I met was Angelo Roselli; he was a great-looking guy, the kind women are drawn to and men trust. A man's man is usually a woman's. Black wavy hair, but with blue eyes, very sun-tanned, good white choppers, dressed like a million bucks, real quiet clothes but gorgeous. Never wore a new pair of shoes, always custom-made, polished, and cracked on top. In all the many years I was to work with and hang around Angie, and no matter how hard I tried, no matter how much time I spent getting duded up, I never saw him that I didn't feel like a slob with nothing fitting right, colors clashing, threads stringing out of sleeves, nose running. There are people like that, born with it like natural athletes. The only time I thought I was coming close was once years after this I ran into Angelo on Broadway and he was wearing a tan gabardine raincoat just like the one I had on and I thought, Now! Nobody could really tell who's better. But we went into Lindy's and when he took off his coat, gave it to the hat-check girl, I saw it was mink-lined. They've got it inside.

I shook hands with him and Red turned to the other man.

"Charley, I'd like you to shake hands with Toddy Fleedhurn. Kid, this is Charley Mayfield."

Charles Mayfield! Good-time Charley Mayfield! A legend I'd heard about all my life. He'd been in the Klondike with Soapy Smith, had cleaned out Australia, what there was there, with Edgar James, and was a hero to all the small-time connies I ever knew who came through South Dakota beating small farmers for a stake to set up a real operation. I did know that the really slick confidence men at that time were working the tubs between Europe and America, and just looking at this man I could tell he was the ocean greyhound's ocean greyhound. He stood up courteously to greet me and I saw that he was at least an inch shorter than my own six feet and that surprised me. I still don't really believe that I was ever taller than the great Good-time Charley Mayfield. But I guess you hear about someone for a long time, you build him up in your mind and that picture never fades. His hair was gray by now, iron gray and heavy; he had to brush it out of his eyes a lot. And they were the kindest eyes I have ever seen. Wore a dark-blue suit, double-breasted with a vest, gold chain on vest with an emblem attached to it which, I learned later, was never the same two nights running. Apparently he had them all: Elks, Masons, Rotarians, and he knew all the handshakes and signs. He even had a Phi Beta Kappa key that I once saw him wear on the old *Mauretania*. I don't know if it was really his or not but he was smart enough to wear it.

He gave me a good firm grip and looked straight into my eyes. I'd have given him my life's savings, if I'd had any, anything.

"Glad to know you, Fleedhurn," he said. All the immaturity I'd been wearing like a gauze cloak slid off my back and I was suddenly grown up. Here was this man, this great legend, and he was shaking my hand in a perfectly lateral way, saying, without words, "You're my equal." Of course I wasn't, but I kept trying to be for many years, playing for a tie till I remembered what Mom wrote in her letter, that I was supposed to compete with no one, just my own potential. All I ever had to become was the best Tod Fleedhurn I could be, but I didn't know that then. And I think you'll agree that I've done a pretty good job of that. I know the old man with the whiskers thinks so, at least his Internal Revenue Service does.

So there I was in Paris, where I'd always wanted to go because French girls are hot, I'd been told, and I was with these great men, had a few bucks in my kick. We had the best meal and champagne and there was music going and I met the most beautiful brunette I'd ever seen. We all went back to Charley's suite which had two bedrooms and they let me take my girl into one of them, Angelo took the other, while Red and Charley talked. Then my girl went home and I fell drunk asleep on the couch.

When I woke up, someone had thrown a blanket on me and it was a little after noon. The other three were in a far corner of the big room, and playing three-handed hearts. I polished off some wild strawberries, brioche, and hot chocolate. (Penny Ann should see me now back there in Rapid City with her hot chocolate. What's the good of progress if the folks you left behind can't see you?) Red asked if I wanted to play some poker.

Play some poker with Good-time Charley Mayfield?! Does a minor-league ballplayer want to shag flies for Ty Cobb? What a break. Listen, at that time I figured that I could improve my fortunes very easily, for I had about $200 (I had squirreled it away while traveling around the world. I was always a fiscal schizoid, trying to look sporty and yet hiding some, and I still am. It never leaves you. At night in "21" I'm calling out "More wine! More wine! Dom Perignon for the whole crowd!" and then the next morning I look at the razor and say "This blade is good for one more shave") and I thought that these fellows would play loose with the kid and all would be well. Within five minutes Angelo had bet $100 into me, I folded, then a half hour later, after I'd built my stack up to even again, Charley bet $200, looked at me in a kindly way, I called and he had me beat. I was Tap City.

"Red, can you let me have fifty dollars?"

"Here, kid." He threw over a handful of chips, uncounted.

I tapped out again shortly.

"Red, could you spare another fifty?"

"Here you go." Again he scooped up a bunch of chips, surely more than fifty's worth, and tossed them to me. Two hands later I got beat by a higher flush and the game was over.

"I owe you a hundred, Red."

"I think you'll find it was a hundred and six."

They all looked at me solemnly till Red suddenly pushed his chair back and laughed; the other two joined him. They'd been having sport with me, just to see how I'd react. Red had told Charley and Angie about me by phone before we met and now they spoke to me about joining them in a business venture, *i.e.*, to work the ships over the Atlantic. Of course I was proud to accept. For these men were all I ever wanted my mentors to be and I give them a great deal of credit for my success.

I studied Charley all I could, because he was like a father to me till the day he went broke, years later, playing the gee-gees and I stopped seeing him, and from him I learned tolerance, wisdom, and self-control (up to a point). Red was not a member of this group; he just cut in for ten per cent of all we'd take for five years for having brought us together. But I had already learned from him to be quick-witted, to live off the land, to make plans, yes, but to be able to switch from the plan at a moment's notice, to juggle time, people, money, everything, all at once. What an operator! And, by the way and above all, survival, which I admire above all, for the only real ruthlessness is self-destruction. With the possible exception of Hitler, Red Sutton had the strongest sense of survival I've ever known and he was a lot more fun to be with. And from Angelo I learned how to get along with people, to like and be liked, to be interested and therefore interesting. I also learned how to wear clothes elegantly but not ostentatiously. He spoke five or six languages in addition to English, could move in all circles. Sometimes he put himself away as an Italian count, sometimes an Argentine playboy, a Spanish millionaire with oil holdings in Persia, anything. And he could compromise with anyone, but never with himself. (Mom's letter again, remember?) Down deep, where he lived, he knew what he wanted to be: a winner.

The business we were in was as follows. We would board a transatlantic ship going east from New York or west from France or England; sometimes one or two of us from France, and the other boarded at England. We always found out from the purser, whom we could take care of, what the passenger list included. That is, we knew who the mark would be. There were certain rules. We never played for a self-made man, we never played for a Jew. Nobody who has respect for earning money will pay it without thinking twice. We never spoke to each other on the ship till we had picked up the mark separately and he had introduced us. I was the youngster from the Middle West whose father had ranches in South Dakota, Montana, and Wyoming (I could discuss all that intelligently, especially with some bum who'd simply inherited his wealth and didn't know anything). Angie was whatever seemed appropriate but always from some foreign country that we could tell the mark had never visited, and Charley was always a Wall Street banker. He even kept an office on the Street as a drop.

About the second or third night of the crossing, which took six days, we'd all have drinks together after dinner and tell tall stories. Played a little bridge, all straight unless the mark was too dumb and then we'd throw a few so he'd be ahead a few dollars. But never much, we were all conservatives, especially Charley, who insisted we keep the game low. We'd make the usual good-natured efforts to pick up the wine bills and on the next to last night before we docked, let's say in New York, assuming we were going west, the mark would insist it was his turn to pay (which it was) and Angelo would claim or want the bill and then I'd say, "No fighting, let's play The Game for it."

They'd all say, "What game?"

"You see," I'd say, "each of us gets dealt one card. And, let's see if I remember this right, yes, the one is the highest card and the two the lowest."

Charley would be taking notes, as if to help his memory but really in case of a rhubarb after. We never said "ace" or "deuce."

"Now then. We each buy matches and we put some of those matches in the pot to bet against, yes that's how it goes."

"Bet against the matches," Charley murmers while he writes.

"I think I played this with the Duke of Buccleuch in Monaco," says Angelo.

"Then what happens?" the Mark asks. He's eager. He's already stacking matches in little piles.

"Well, whoever has the highest card in front of him bets against the pot. Any amount up to the size of the pot."

"Oh, I remember this game," says the Mark. "I'm sure I played it with my nursie when I was a child."

"Of course. Then the dealer gives him another card, and if he beats the card, he takes the amount he bet from the pot. If he loses or ties, why, he puts that amount in. And whoever wins the pot, he gets to buy the round of drinks."

How do you like the word "ties" there? It's the key word.

Swell. So then we make each match worth a dollar and the Mark wins 1,400 or 1,500 bucks, no money at all to three swell millionaires like us. And he goes back to his stateroom thinking he's on to a good thing. Just as every greedy son of a bitch in the world thinks when he's won a few bucks.

However.

The next night, last before port, we play again. Everybody seems lucky, gets good cards, betting the pot but then losing. Do you know how fast a pot jumps to real big dough with a few double-ups like that? And now it's the Mark's turn and he deals the four cards around. Ending with an ace in front of himself.

"I'll bet the pot," he says, holding the deck, which naturally is a cold one we'd put in for this deal. He's got flecks of greed all over his face.

"Just a minute, Mr. Mark." Charley holds the dealer's arm. "There's quite a good deal of money in there. You don't want to be a hog, do you?" But now you can't stop him. He's known it all along. He's been watching the markers being thrown in for all those pot bets. Well, sir, guess what he deals himself? Right.

Another ace. His face is usually quite white as Angelo counts through the markers and matches.

"A hundred and twenty-eight thousand dollars." Or sixty-four or whatever. So the Mark's marker goes in for that; Charley, with his honest gray hair and king in front of him, also bets the pot but of course he wins. The next day, wherever we dock, Charley turns the Mark's check into cash, we divvy after holding out Red's split, and everybody's happy. Oh, maybe the Mark isn't so happy, but he has learned something more about himself, and isn't knowledge power? Of course it is. Knowledge and a few bucks.

We made three or four trips a year riding the old *Homeric*, the *Mauretania*, all the great liners of Cunard, White Star, the German ships, French, Italian, the whole bunch. We almost never failed to connect unless there were too many combinations working the same ship. Then we either laid off or made split deals. In between jobs we lived the high life: went to resorts, usually on a vacation basis but always with eyes opened for business. Of course we all didn't always travel together, but each of us knew where the others were in case he ran into a sucker. And so much wonderful stuff brushed off on me because the people we played for were all gentlemen and mostly college grads.

This was the twenties; Babe Ruth, Jack Dempsey, Helen Morgan, Harry Richman, we knew them all. The paper money was big and beautiful greenbacks and gold and always plenty. Race tracks, ball games, night clubs. Can you imagine what this all meant to a kid who thought they stamped "Small Time" on his ass when he was born? Paris, London, New York, Saratoga, Palm Beach; great grub, great duds. And if you think that somewhere there was an emptiness gnawing at the heart, forget it. It was FUN, and it was GREAT, and what do the words "Sitting on Top of the World" mean to you as a person?

But there's always someone around to explain that you've missed the real boat, and I always listen.

10

Now it was 1937, September, and we had made an important score. Charley hadn't been in on this one; he was in Havana trying to set up a payoff store. But Angie and I were still together along with an Australian connie I had found when we started playing for each other that summer in Bar Harbor. His name was Covington Fulton and it was his real name, so that helped. A tall stooped man, oh I'll say he went six foot three, about sixty-five but he looked good and ageless, perpetual sun tan, farsighted blue eyes, and put himself away as a sheep rancher. Just before I boarded the old *Normandie*, I got word that Red Sutton had been killed in a knife fight in Paris and that made me feel like hell. I gritted my teeth, determined to make a good score this crossing. Win one for Red.

The first night at sea I went scouting in the bar and was talking to an Englishman I had just picked up when I noticed Covington come in. He spotted me, didn't say anything, then he saw the gee I was with and started out of the room. But too late. The Englisher jumped off his seat and ran after him.

"Cov! Cov Fulton! It's I, Harry Ashcroft."

Cov smiled sickly, they shook hands and then came back to me at the bar.

"You know, we haven't met at all," said the Englishman to me. "I'm Lord Carlton, but do call me Harry. And this is my friend Covington Fulton."

Well, Cov told me later when we got a moment in the men's room, that he had beaten this guy on a short con in Palm Beach the previous year, relieving him of $15,000. So he didn't exactly think he should show his face this time, but the mark, whose father, incidentally, had left him £10,000,000, didn't feel a thing and was delighted to see Cov, who, let's face it, was a master anyway. Very personable. Later on, the mark managed to meet Angelo, introduce him to us and at the dock we had a check for 128 big ones that Milord went for and he was thrilled to do it. So were we.

Angelo and I went to the Diamond Horseshoe our second night back to celebrate. After the show, one of the girls from the dance line came over to the table. Angie always surprised me, he knew everybody: gamblers, millionaires, high-society ladies, and show people and knew them all well, on his terms. When he asked her to get a date for me, my life changed again, this time for good.

She went backstage and came back with a girl who made my heart leap. I'd noticed her during the show; she'd been by far the best dancer, with an exquisite body and every movement graceful. I could hardly believe my luck. She had long dark hair, big brown eyes that looked straight at you, and a kind of solemn look till she smiled and that was a sunrise. It was a most infrequent smile and I kept trying to get it. When she walked, it seemed to be on her toes; I mean she glided. Her name was Matilda Summers. Matilda Summers.

Now before I get into this, let me tell you about the Depression. People who had been floating high before were now floating out of windows. Families were living in shacks by the Hudson and on every corner somebody, trying to feed his family and to keep some dignity by not begging, was selling apples. Money was an emotion. It's not that having money means a good life, but being completely without it or the hope of it is a Chamber of Horrors. For the first time people thought of food not by taste but by its nutritional value. They learned that sleep could re-create the energy that food used to take care of and they slept longer. People, young and old, didn't think of what they wanted to do, how to express themselves, about a place in the stream of life but just how to get a job and keep it, whatever the hours were. I realized all this when I began hanging around with Matilda and her friends.

I fell hard for her. Took to picking her up every night after the last show, having a little supper, usually at some all-night drugstore or hash joint, then taking her home to where she lived on West 87th Street. The fourth time I picked her up I stayed at the apartment with her and I never looked back. I'd never known anything like what holding her in my arms felt because I was truly in love. For the first, last, and only time. When we got through making love, I corked right off to sleep and woke up to the smell of bacon cooking. It was three in the afternoon. I had never slept so late and so well, and I followed my nose into the kitchen where Matty was cooking up a storm.

"There's your orange juice," she said, pointing to the kitchen table. I sat down. "And I have bacon and eggs for you plus toast lightly buttered by the hand that held the hand that held my bottom last night. I hope you don't mind."

"I think I'm in love with you."

"You'd better be." She leaned down to kiss my nose. "Now you pour the coffee."

Best day of my life. It was Sunday so she had no show that night and about six o'clock friends of hers started showing up and over the next couple of weeks I found that her place was a drop-in joint for a whole group of people, the kind I'd never known. Because Matty loved to learn, to get information, opinions; she was an intellectual sponge. And Sunday was her big day.

That first day was an amazement to me, with my sheltered experience of scufflers and marks only. There were a couple of Communists there, one was a little fellow who worked for the *Daily Worker* as a writer and the other a schoolteacher, a great big guy. The little writer, who wasn't as gentle as the other Commie, had his girl friend with him, a dancer between Broadway shows. Then there was a woman about forty-odd who was a psychoanalyst; she talked a lot, my God she talked a lot, and forcefully. There was a poet showed up about nine o'clock who didn't have much to say at all and a black musician who arrived with his horn case and even a priest in a black mohair suit, turned-around collar, and all. I remember saying to Matilda, when she intro'd me to him, "You've got it all now, honey, radicals, doctor, trumpet man, and now you have a sky pilot."

"Is that what they call you?" she asked the priest. "I never heard that before."

"Why yes," he said, "they call us that in the air corps."

Baloney. They were called that everywhere. He was one of those people who just don't want to admit they're ignorant of anything. A lot of them give you directions when you're on the road. I put him down as a phony right away and that made me feel better because the way the conversation had been going I knew I was over my head. Not drowning, but definitely over my head.

I got into the conversation just once in about eight hours. Once the poet mentioned something about gamblers and the lady psychoanalyst said that gambling was the childish desire to get something for nothing. I told her that all the gamblers I'd ever known were never satisfied till they lost everything, that I'd never heard a gambler say, when I tried to get him away from a table, anything other than "Wait'll I get rid of this century note" or whatever the amount was. She said that Freud had a whole chapter on it and that's the way it was, the way she said. And I offered that maybe Freud was wrong. She got shrill and told me I didn't know what the hell I was talking about and I shouldn't discuss things I didn't understand and all that. O.K. Then things started to open up more because most of the people had brought jugs of wine and it was all passed around. Some more jumpers had shown from Matty's dance line and one of them was bitching that every time she had a date the guy tried to jump on her bones right away and why were men such beasts.

"In the entire animal kingdom, my dear," said the analyst, who was getting back her confidence, "the female is always sexually the aggressor. It is always up to us. We come into a room, and what we choose, we take." Hopeful she was, because I'd have to make the price eight to five against her getting laid anywhere. She was not exactly a knockout. I think she shaved her forehead.

"The Greeks knew everything." The big Communist, the schoolteacher, had been quiet for hours until now. I liked him; he talked with a Brooklyn accent. "They have a legend about Zeus and Hera sitting up on

Olympus and he says to her, 'Let's rip one off'; this is a liberal translation."

"That's because you're a liberal," said the little Commie, who was smashed and trying to grope his lady.

"Thank you. Anyway Hera says, 'You men, that's all you think of, sex, sex, sex.' So Zeus says, 'You girls like it too.' 'We do not,' says Hera, 'we do it just for you men, to make you feel good.' So Zeus suggests that they bring one of those shepherd boys they always have on tap up to Olympus, which they do. They tell him he'll be a man for one week and a broad for one week and he should fuck all he can as each and then come back. Which, being a good God-fearing shepherd boy, he does. 'Which way'd you like it best?' they ask him. 'As a woman,' he replies truthfully. So Hera struck his eyes out."

"That's just a Greek legend," said the little Commie.

"Hmmm," said his girl friend.

And on went the conversations. Seemed to me everyone was hustling everyone else. The two Commies were saying the world was going down the drain unless we all joined the party. The analyst said nothing would help unless we all, the world, that is, got psychoanalyzed, and of course the priest was hustling his all-time favorite, Jesus, in whom we had to put our trust. But there must have been twenty people in the joint by midnight and pretty soon they paired off somehow and I was alone again with my love. That's what I believed in.

I checked out of my hotel that week and moved in with Matty. First time I ever actually lived with a woman and it was wonderful. Of course she was always after me to improve myself too.

"You should read more, Toddy."

"Don't you like me?"

"I love you, darling."

"Why is it that the people who love you always want to change you?"

I must say she did put her money where her mouth was. She read all the time and was always taking classes; not only dance classes and singing and acting, but courses in English literature and psychology and economics and God knows what else. So I had to take all this from her especially since I wasn't doing anything at all. Our profession had fallen off with the Depression and to tell the truth I was resisting going off with any of the connies as long as I still had some loot and Matilda.

"How're you going to find out who you are, honey," she'd say, "if you don't have a feeling of what went before from all those wonderful writers who are giving themselves to you through their work?"

I have a strong sense of duty, always have had, so I read all the books she laid on me in the next few weeks. I read through everything I could get from and about Freud, Marx, and Einstein, the three people who changed the world most in the last century. (Three German Jews. Makes you think, doesn't it?) Then I tried to improve myself by reading biographies and got hung up on Dr. Albert Schweitzer, who was then also Matilda's favorite. I think it was all giving me the brain fever because one night while waiting for her to get through, which wasn't till 4:00 A.M., I wandered into a joint called the Savannah Club where I got smashed out of my mind, a bad idea when one is depressed. I was really getting away from all those damn intellectuals in the house. Got to the club about eleven and the next thing I knew it was three o'clock in the morning and I was sitting at a table in this crib, a place I'd never been before and where they didn't know me, with a bottle of rotgut wine they called champagne in an ice bucket, one hooker with her leg over mine and another nibbling at my ear. I called for the check. It was $110, and when I looked for the money in my kick I found only a ten-dollar bill. I could see the proprietor already talking to a large party at the door who I knew was the bouncer because he looked like he could break your leg with two fingers. I didn't know what to do, so I thought, What would Dr. Albert Schweitzer do in this case? He is a great man, so based on all the reading I, Tod Fleedhurn, have done about him, I will figure that out and then I, Tod Fleedhurn, will do it.

But what I couldn't figure out was what the hell Dr. Albert Schweitzer was doing in the Savannah Club at three in the morning. While I was trying to put that in place, they relieved me of my sawbuck, took me out in the alley, and beat the shit out of me. I landed one good shot and that was all because I was too drunk, and at my best that bouncer could have killed me. Well, he figured to be better than most; it was his whole life, beating people up. He wasn't reading about great men and all that. While he was kicking me I was thinking, I guess I really did leave the house without much money. Those girls couldn't have rolled me, because if they had, they wouldn't be killing me here in the alley. So my last thought before flaking out was one of success that I hadn't been robbed because I'd hate to be a mark.

I was out only a few minutes. Then I pulled myself up and started walking around, really just quietly crazy. I didn't know what I was doing or who I was. Not a nickel in my pocket to call Matilda, even if I'd wanted to, or to get a cup of coffee and there I was on 4th Street, miles from Matilda on West 87th Street where I didn't want to go anyway.

"Would you rather be full of fear or full of guilt?" I asked myself. The answer took ten blocks.

"Full of fear!" I shouted out loud. "I've been full of guilt all my life." It didn't occur to me that there could be other choices. I started shivering when I thought of all the fear I was full of; that shivering along with the dried blood on my face must have made me a lovely sight when I walked into the Weylin Hotel on 54th Street where I knew Alvin Meyer, the night clerk. He was a nice guy, even though queer as a three-dollar bill.

"My God, what happened, Mr. Fleedhurn?"

"I hit a taxi, Alvin. Can you put me into a room?"

"Sure. Here's the key to 1104, your old room."

That was a mistake. I had lived in that room from time to time before I'd met Matilda and between excursions. Always had partied it up pretty good there; the memory was all delight but now it was empty delight. I couldn't hold on to a thing, even friends. And there is nothing so debilitating as a life of acquaintances. Then I started thinking about the last three years with Matilda and her friends and I couldn't stop weeping.

She was right. I hadn't accomplished anything, ever. But what she didn't know was that I couldn't accomplish anything. As I told you, this was a time when money was an emotion, that's all you thought of. The prime accomplishment was to have a job. There was no such thing as quitting because you weren't satisfied; you just could not be out of a job.

And I didn't even know what job I was out of. I thought about all this while I was wiping the dried blood off my face, trying to make myself look presentable. I thought that I was completely useless, and I was weak, yes weak. I had always thought I was all right, and I was even happy sometimes, sad at the proper times, tried to be nice to people and genuinely like them, even when I was trimming them. But I realized then, as I crawled out on the eleventh-floor ledge because it was all too close there in the room now, that I had an emotional hernia and all my feelings were pouring through.

By the time I got a few feet out on the ledge and was sitting there, my legs over the side, trying to think things through, it had somehow become eight o'clock in the morning and there were people on 54th Street going to work.

Someone down there must have seen me because the next thing I knew Alvin Meyer was leaning out the window of 1104 and calling to me.

"Mr. Fleedhurn, what are you doing to me? Oh my God, if you fall, it's my ass."

"What about your ass, Alvin?"

"Oh, I knew I should never have let you in, the awful way you looked, I knew it. Please, please come back inside."

"Go away, Alvin."

And he did. I think it's the first time anyone ever did exactly what I told them, a heady feeling for me while it lasted. I couldn't figure out why I should go back in, I couldn't figure out why I should drop eleven floors to the ground either. I was indecisive and that is hell.

I saw people down below pointing and shouting, though I couldn't hear what they were yelling up at me. I thought, What the hell am I going to go on living for? I don't accomplish anything, Matilda is right. There's a mosaic around but I don't fit into it and what's more important, I don't want to fit into it. Her two Communist friends were always trying to get me to enlist in the party, but that didn't fit me, I knew that. That priest who always came around and wanted me to "embrace the Catholic church. You won't be sorry." And that woman psychoanalyst who believed my salvation, everybody's, lay on the couch. They all wanted me to join something and all I wanted to do was to be let alone. Thinking this I brightened because I certainly was alone out there now.

"Why don't ye came in, me bye, and have a drink wit' me?" A cop was leaning out my window, holding a bottle of booze and a glass.

"No, thank you, officer."

"Ah, nothin's so bad that a jar with a friend isn't better than the end." He faked pouring some in the glass, drank from it and smacked his lips, wiping them with his sleeve.

"Think of yer loved ones, me bye." I did and slipped a couple of inches nearer the end of the ledge. The cop pulled his head in and I heard him talking to Alvin. I went on thinking about how swell it was to be alone with yourself and how much better it was than being lonely, which is being without yourself. But I couldn't yet rid myself of the feeling that I was of no value, unworthy; it was gnawing at me like a hunger. In fact I was hungry. When you see me now, with all I've done, my millions, those thoughts seem unbelievable, ridiculous, but I had them.

"Officer, don't crawl out here, please." The dope had taken off his blouse, gun belt and all, and was making his fat way towards me. "You're making a fool of yourself." He was an awfully fat cop for that narrow ledge.

"How would ye like a nice cup of cocoa, me bye?"

"Now why would I have crawled out on an eleventh-story ledge for a cup of cocoa?" He almost slipped and got red in the face pulling himself back on. "Ooh, that was a close one, officer. Watch how you crawl."

"I'm crawlin' the way I want to crawl! Now are you goin' to come back in the room or am I goin' to have to take ye in?" He was moving pretty fast now so I moved along the ledge too, away from him.

"Watch it, officer, that's the tricky part, getting around that pillar there."

"You watch it, you lousy little son of a . . ."

I did and what a splat he made. Well, I thought, he can't say I didn't warn him. I noticed that some of the people on the street were shaking their fists up at me. Then I heard a little commotion back at my window and there was Matilda, leaning out the window saying something, tears streaming down her cheeks. I never knew she could cry like that.

Matilda had brought the priest and her analyst friend with her and they tried talking to me, but of course none of them would go out on the ledge like that dumb cop. I didn't pay much attention to any of them because I was getting involved with the growing crowd on the street. I was shouting, "What's the matter with all of you? Haven't you ever seen anyone on a ledge before? I'm where you all should be. I'm here for you." Which was a lie, because I was there for myself only.

The head doctor and the priest had both pulled in and I heard them arguing, voices were raised. Then Matilda leaned out again.

"Please come in, Tod darling, please come in. I'll do anything you want."

"But what do you want, Matty?"

"All I want is your happiness." Sounded just like my mother.

"Well, you can't have it. It's mine." Then I knew what I did want, crawled a few more feet to the window of the next room which I found empty, raised it, went in, and called room service.

"Could you send up a pot of steaming cocoa, please?"

But they were all out of cocoa by then.

Then the police ran me in, charged me with murder second degree. Mr. Amos "Wingy" Loeffler, our one-armed lawyer, had to arrange for $5,000 bail and the newspapers had a field day. COP KILLER FREED ran one *Daily News* headline; another was DRUNKEN LOVE NEST PARTY ENDS IN TRAGEDY and so on. Naturally they found out about Norman and Lester, the two Communists, who hung around the house all the time, so now I was pictured as holding a bomb with a lighted fuse in one hand and poor Matilda's virginity in the other. Of course I was sorry about that cop, but he was the one who had crawled out there and he fell, he wasn't pushed. But this was 1941 and the feeling for authority was high. They had some dame writing pieces every day about it, about "why isn't this able-bodied man in the armed forces?" and all that.

I came to preliminary trial to see if they should try to pin anything on me. I certainly didn't want to go to jail but I was so depressed I didn't care too much. My picture had been all over the papers and my career as an ocean greyhound was at a standstill, to say the least. Neither Angelo nor Cov Fulton nor any of the other connies had made contact with me, and I understood that of course. I was alone in this thing and I didn't want to bring shame on our house, so to speak.

I was alone, yes, and that just meant that all the decisions were mine, a heady feeling, and that I had to think fast on my feet, act with assurance in all matters. So all that started to sharpen me up.

We went before the judge, a certain Judge Jeremiah Mulcahy, on a Tuesday morning, and the prosecutor, a man in his middle years with spots on his vest, made an impassioned plea to put me in jail. That I had been the cause of the demise of one Patrolman McGloin, a brave family man and all the rest. Mulcahy just listened, nodding once in a while. Took no notes. Then Wingy Loeffler got up and said that I had been temporarily aberrated and should get medical attention in some facility and all that, that I wasn't responsible and he could bring the necessary head doctors to the trial, if there was one, to testify to that fact. The prosecutor spoke again to say that I hadn't been legally insane and that he would bring his own head doctors to the court to prove before the law that I had been sane.

So there I was: the state wanting me in durance vile and my own attorney saying I should be in a laughing academy. Bad spot. But at times like this, when they close in on me, I'm at my most dangerous.

"How is your client going to plead?" Judge Jeremiah Mulcahy asked. I got to my feet before Wingy could say anything.

"Guilty, Your Honor," I said. Wingy went into shock.

"Guilty?" asked Mulcahy.

"What I mean, sir, is . . . aren't we all guilty, I mean, in the larger sense? Here we are in the midst of a world conflagration, and what are we all doing about it? Nothing."

"This man is . . ." The D.A. jumped up.

"Leave him alone." When Mulcahy said that, I knew I had him. "Go on."

"All I mean, Your Honor, is here we are, our country helping everyone else, and is any of us doing enough? I do think we are all a little guilty, that's all I mean."

"Let's all go to my chambers." He whacked the gavel, walked off, and the D.A., his assistant, along with Wingy and me, followed him to his chambers. I knew where he was headed in his conversation because I had headed him there. All he wanted to know was how come I wasn't in the army. I told him I'd been deferred because of a trick knee; I saw no reason to tell him that I had paid the medical clerk $200 to put the right news on the report so that I would be deferred.

"I am not without some influence, Fleedhurn. Suppose I could get you accepted by the armed forces. Would you want that?"

"I'd want that more than anything on earth," I said. I meant it too. I figured a year in the army was a hell of a lot better than time in the can or the funny farm. "I'd pay $200 to be in Uncle Sam's army."

"I don't think you'll have to, son. That isn't the way things are done in this land of ours."

"But, Your Honor," the D.A. objected, "this man has no visible means of support other than gaming, he was the cause of the death of a noble policeman, and he should stand trial."

"Your Honor"—now Wingy thought he had to protect me—"my client is not guilty of anything because he isn't competent. As for the armed forces, he was legally deferred because of an injured knee."

"I think, whatever his background has been"—here Mulcahy smiled at me benevolently like he was admitting me into a church; I looked back at him with my most open face—"that he will make a good soldier, and I daresay that when his country calls, he will, like every red-blooded American, run, walk, or limp forward."

"Oh, that's more true today than it ever was." I breathed out the words just loud enough for the Judge to hear.

I had Mulcahy pegged perfectly. He was one of those red-hot secondhand patriots. He thought that no one else did enough for his country, so sure enough three days later he had fixed it with one of his pals on the draft board to accept the undersigned and I found myself at Fort Dix a buckass private in the United States Infantry on September 30, 1941. With all charges dropped.

At first it was all wonderful. I didn't have to worry about some person or other telling me what to do, *everyone* told me what to do.

I was shipped down to Fort Bragg after induction and on the train they put us two in a lower berth, one noncom in an upper, and commissioned officers got rooms. I thought, Toddy, this won't do at all, so when I got to Bragg and they took a look at my high AGCT score, and asked me if I wanted to apply for officer candidate school, I jumped at it. Then everything happened at once. The Japs bombed Pearl Harbor, we declared war, and I was a second lieutenant on my way to North Africa.

When I look back on it all now, I can't believe it. In North Africa I got myself involved in a holding action because our company commander got himself killed and, what the hell, I had to take over. I had absolutely no choice but to have us fight and we got lucky and I got hit on the ass and the Colonel put me in for a D.S.C. Like I had done something brave. I had to shoot at them, they were shooting at me. When I left the hospital, where I won close to $3,800 playing poker, they gave me a company of my own, so I made captain which, with overseas pay and all, wasn't too bad a deal.

Went into combat again and this time picked up a Bronze Star before we all got shipped over to England.

I was trying to figure out a way to get back to the States, figured I'd done my tour and all, when the Commanding General told me that he'd send me back if I wanted but that if I'd stay for the invasion he'd promote me to battalion exec, which called for a majority. At the time, I was boffing a great English girl named Ann, at the Windmill, an actress, so I had no desire now to leave England and I thought those major's leaves would look just fine. I made major, went over on D-day, stayed long enough to pick up some more fruit salad, then was sent back to England for States rotation. Found out that Ann was preggers about three months. And since I had been gone almost seven months and I have this high I.Q. I told you about, quick like a bunny I figured she'd made a new pal. I thought I might as well go back to New York and see my Matilda, who had been writing me regularly and there was no Dear John in the bunch.

I landed in New York April of 1945 and though I'd just had four years of everybody telling me what to do, I felt pretty good because I'd always done what I wanted to do anyway and things had worked out. I was a goddam hero—what with back pay and everything I had by now about seven grand in my pocket and I was alive which is worth twice that, give or take a couple of hundred dollars.

Let me tell you what happens when some son of a bitch, let's say for instance, gets thrown into the crucible of enemy fire, sees his pals killed at his feet, etc. He then becomes a son of a bitch who has been under enemy fire, has seen his pals killed at his feet, etc. It doesn't do a thing for you. What I mean is, I took up just where I had left off.

Matilda was now working in the chorus of a

Broadway show, so I moved right in with her. I looked around but couldn't find any of the guys I had actually worked with, just some Johnny-come-latelies whom I didn't feel much like being with. Also those four years in the army, leading men, making decisions, had changed me a lot. I felt like striking out on my own or at least trying a new graft. Mostly I wanted to be my own man, now I felt I was ready. While Matilda was jumping around the stage, I took to walking around the city, getting familiar with it again and with myself. I was getting very close to myself, close to the point where I would be free because I could feel responsible. Not guilty, as I used to feel, when I first met Matty (and I hadn't even known it till she pointed it out to me; she and some of those damn authors she made me read), but responsible. And responsibility is the essence of freedom; guilt is an indulgence, an arrogance. It was all going great, till one night when I was walking down 42nd Street between Fifth and Sixth Avenues, in front of Stern Brothers.

13

It was about ten o'clock, a bright moonlit night, and I was moseying west toward the Shubert Theatre where Matty was working but I was in no particular hurry because the show didn't break till eleven. Fellow had a pitch going there on the sidewalk with a pretty good-sized telescope, headed up over Bryant Park to the moon. A few people were hanging around listening to him sell a look at the moon and astrological charts and so I joined the tip, just to be amused, you know the feeling—here was a small-time connie working, I could feel superior. And he wasn't bad either, not at all. Then he said,

". . . now we know that the body is eighty-five per cent water. And we know that the moon controls the tide, so . . ."

He owned me. Again I was owned. I could feel dat ol' dabbil moon pulling me here and there. I bought the chart and could hardly wait to pick up Matty.

"You are generous to a fault, yet shrewd and practical in business matters," it said. Oh of course, so true. This was a good month for me to have an affair of the heart, but I should be careful because I was sensitive and could be hurt. Matilda took an extremely dim view of all this when we were at Harold's Show Spot that night after her performance.

"Toddy, darling," she said between bites of her sandwich, "surely you, you of all people, don't believe in Fate, Destiny, 'It is written . . .' and all that garbage."

"Of course not! But suppose I'm all wrong. Suppose there is a plan, a grand plan, shouldn't we try to find out what it is? And where could it be written better than in the stars?"

"In your eyes, dumbbell." She leaned over and gave me a kiss on the ear. She always got lovey-dovey when I was on something else.

"Suppose all this had happened before; there've been eleven atom bombs, the world blown up ten times already. Then what?"

"Then order me another beer." She cuddled up to me on the seat in the booth.

"There must be something that influences us all, something that went before. Napoleon was an emperor because he was short. Suppose his mommy and his daddy hadn't been tiny persons, would he have become an emperor?"

"Well, there've been tall emperors and short waiters. Louie"—she indicated our waiter, who was putting down the beer—"is only five foot two. And he ain't no emperor."

"Oh, what the hell, Matilda," I groaned, "you're no help."

"How'd you like to get your plow scraped, buddy?" She pinched me and we went home. Where she was some help but it was all more mysterious than ever.

In the next few weeks I looked around for something to do but was still almost obsessed with trying for self-improvement through astrology which moved me into yoga, other metaphysics, and finally right back to reading biographies in an attempt to learn from my masters. You'd have thought that experience with Albert Schweitzer who let me down in the Savannah Club would have given me religion, but I went back. Of course I never, never do know when to quit something, because then I'm afraid I'm a quitter, or to press on beating a dead horse which would make me a dope. But I kept going.

I got Rupert Hughes's biography of George Washington and then found some newspaper articles in the public library on microfilm about Babe Ruth, and also read up on Edgar Degas, the only painter whose work I feel really close to. Well, as you know, Geo W had a habit of going into the slave quarters and boffing the little black girls there, the Bambino drank a quart of whiskey a day, and Degas was very punishing to women. I felt I should do likewise, as a start. The fact that I wasn't founding any countries, hitting baseballs, or painting pictures didn't occur to me. I had to find out if this system worked.

So one Wednesday afternoon, while Matty was doing her matinee at the theater, I stayed home and started to hit the bottle just like the old Sultan of Swat would have done, I thought. Meanwhile, I was watching Mary Lou, our colored maid, who was dusting up the place and getting prettier and prettier with every drink I took. I tried to think how George would have handled it, what he would have said. I was sprawled on the couch and she had to come near me to go over the coffee table.

"Come here, you little vixen." I made a grab for her skirt but missed, almost fell off the damn couch, actually.

"Why, Mist' Fleedhurn, whatchyou doin'?"

"I'm going to kiss you, Mary Lou, that's what I'm adoin.'"

"Now you behave yourself, Mist' Fleedhurn."

I couldn't get my arms around her. First place, she was quite small and wiry, and then too I was drunk. This wasn't working. Then I thought of Degas. Eddie like to beat up on them and, I surmised, they liked to be beat up on. That's what I was doing wrong, just trying to make ordinary love. Which only served to cheapen me, which only made me low, in the eyes of this dusky serving girl.

"You want a little of this, do you, my dear?" and I whacked her a good one across her tight little ass.

Well, she took that mop handle, shoved it in my eye, and, with the same move somehow continued, turned it all around to bop me on the head with the mop. When Matilda got home she found me with a black eye and a lump on the noggin that wouldn't quit. Mary Lou was applying cold compresses and I was miserable.

"You poor darling, what happened?" Matty ran over to the couch where I was lying.

"I fell down."

"Ah been tryin' to help him, Miz Matty, but all he calls for is you. 'Where's Matty,' he say, 'where's Matty.'" I fixed her with a one-eyed baleful look while she tried to stop giggling. Then Mary Lou ran into the other room wiping her eyes as if crying, while Matilda took up the cold towel for the eye and head sloshing.

Well, I thought, that's why Geo Washington and the Bambino and Degas were great men. Or did I overreach myself? I mean, none of them tried to do it all.

But still, I felt a whole lot better the next day because I was rid of the illusion that I could pattern myself after anyone else and there is nothing as exhausting as illusion. I know that and you know that.

Leroy, fix me another one with not too much soda this time, and a little of that cracked crab we've got in the fridge. I'm going good now.

14

Matilda and I had a nice long, adult, sensible talk the next day on the subject of my possibly going around the bend if I didn't start working. She thought I'd fallen down because I was drunk and she did not approve and of course I couldn't tell her the truth. I certainly agreed with her, so I took Wingy Loeffler to lunch and asked him to look around for a good proposition for me to go into because he had a lot of good connections.

A week later, he introduced me to a fellow named Bert Larrabee who had leases on oil land in Oklahoma, about 2,500 acres' worth, but was too undercapitalized to market them or do anything else. To put it another way, he was Tap City, all but locked out of his hotel room. He also had a list he had bought from an old bucket-shop operator out of Fresno who had made enough money to retire. Larrabee offered to go partners with me, fifty-fifty right down the line if I backed us to the tune of a decent car that would take us across the country and get us started selling in California, where the client list was from. You know, Fresno, Tulare, Visalia, all around L.A., of widows and retired people who'd possibly be interested and had the wherewithal. And he had a hell of a good pitch to go on which I did check.

"I do not tell you that we will discover oil," we could say. "No human can promise that. We can tell you, however, that the Rockefeller interests are drilling just north and west of the boundaries of this property here on the map." Etc. etc. And we would jocularly agree that old John D and his heirs didn't get rich making too many mistakes. And all that and so on.

This took only a few days to iron out and then I broached the subject to Matilda, whose show was closing anyway.

"What will we *do* out there, Tod?"

"There are no wild Indians, honey. This is 1946."

"Oh, I know that. I mean, we're both sidewalk people and that's all country, I hear."

"It's a lot bigger than Rapid City. The point is I've got a chance to go into business for myself, something you've always wanted me to do, and, yes, that I've wanted to do." I was selling now. On a roll. "And let's face it, Matty, our whole relationship could use a shot in the arm. After all, a man has to be his own man before he can be any woman's man and since a man is only what he does, I have to do this thing, to express myself."

"Do you mean to tell me"—her gorgeous eyes widened in astonishment or admiration or both—"that selling bucket-shop oil stock is a form of self-expression? And besides, what the hell is wrong with our relationship? Don't you love me?"

"Of course I do." I put my arm around her and squeezed. She usually liked that. "I love you completely. But completely does not necessarily mean forever. Everything is in change. If I do not do something creative, the little that is beautiful in me may wither and die. And then our love could wither also."

"And die." She looked at me thoughtfully. "You

know, Tod, someday God is going to strike you dead, just to keep the franchise here on Earth. But I swear, there is something marvelous in you. To follow a path like the one you just followed, not knowing whither it may leadeth, e'en tho' the morrow may disaster bring—" she threw her arms around me now, kissed me, leaned back and smiled at me; oh, she knew me well—"takes the guts of a blind burglar. And I'd follow you, sirrah, down the mouth of a cannon." She laughed and kissed me again. "I would that."

The next day Bert Larrabee and I worked out the details, as many as we could. Of course it was all a handshake deal—in our profession it had to be like that—except that he did sign over 1,250-odd acres to me, exactly half the action. That was signed in Wingy's office. During the week we looked at cars, finally bought a good Buick that was only a year old but clean—I insisted on that—and I also advanced Bert a thousand dollars for walking-around money, to get out of his hotel, etc.

I didn't know the man well, but I tried to check him out a bit from a couple of stock nicks I knew. Nobody seemed to know whether he was Canadian or not but apparently he'd made quite a lot of money up there in Canada till he ran afoul of the Northwest Mounted Police. I never found out what the charge was but it must have been Opinionation, First Degree. I never met a man who asked so few questions as Bert Larrabee, but I found that all out later, on the trip. He was a baldheaded guy, walked with a good carriage, like a soldier, clear eye, firm handclasp, and polite. Altogether, he struck me as a man who knew his job, our job. So we left within a week.

What I did not know about him, also, was that his real ambitions were to be a witness at an important trial and to make a hundred million dollars in a crap game. I found out that first part on the road and the last in Las Vegas.

All the way across the country this son of a bitch was telling me his opinions. He didn't bother Matilda too much, because since he and I split the driving we were always in the front while Matty rode in the back and she had a marvelous time. She had never been west of Philadelphia and she loved looking out at the farmland, the mountains, the streams, everything. I was happy just seeing things through her eyes.

But this bum next to me: whatever we looked at reminded him of some other place he ascertained Matty and I had never seen, and then he would tell us why his place was better. Then he would tell me unless I visited that place I hadn't really been anywhere. At mealtime he was another Gayelord Hauser, but always as a counterpuncher. By that I mean he'd wait for me to order and no matter what it was, he'd shake his head as if to say "How can you do this to your precious body" and then he would order something else but ever so carefully. If I asked for meat, he'd order fish; if I ordered fish, he'd go for "the New York steak, medium rare, but please, no butter on it and cut the fat *before* you cook it." Didn't matter what he ordered because he always sent it back at least once anyway. Kept the kitchen on its toes and the fact that he may still be alive today and not lying with a meat cleaver in his skull can only be attributed to the large number of culinary masochists all over the world.

I remember one morning in Laramie, Wyoming, after we had, for the only time on the trip, I swear it, and only because we thought we had earned a little party for ourselves, got blind drunk the night before. At least I had. All I could remember that morning was opening my eyes from where I was lying in a gutter outside the Antlers Café, lying in a pool of vomit, I may say, and seeing a whole cowboy looming over me.

"Somebody's had a little too much Christmas," I heard him say. The labor of figuring out which month we actually were in, which was September, enabled me to come to life at last and get in the sack at 3:30 A.M.

So when I got to the breakfast nook at eight o'clock to meet the others and get a good start on the day, I looked like I had been slept in. Matty was O.K., I guess, but I couldn't really tell because she wouldn't talk to me, indeed turned her face away. I was riddled with alcoholic guilt and honeycombed with anxiety. About everything.

"Should never mix your drinks, old boy," Bert said.

I'll kill him, I thought. I'll kill him just by thinking I'll kill him.

"Your breath smells like a sewer," Matty said. Her face was still turned away but she held out a pack of Pep-O-Mint Life Savers. I reached for one but then shook my head and turned it down. I was thinking, It's all sugar. Pits the teeth. No good. Juju, juju. I was afraid of everything. I noticed Bert glancing at his watch and making one of the notes he always made in his little notebook.

"What the hell are you doing now?" I asked.

"Always like to know where I am and when. Supposing somebody, for the sake of example, got shot in here? And I were called as a witness? 'How do you know the exact time the murder was committed and where you were?' the prosecutor will sneer, and I shall reply simply, 'Because I wrote it all down' and then I whip out my notebook and tell him I was seated thirty-six feet from the front door at precisely 8:14 A.M."—here he consulted his watch again—"and I've got him knocked on his ass."

"Not if you're the one who's murdered," I said under my breath. I was searching the menu for something that my poor fragile little system could take without my falling dead at my own feet. Toast? The whiter the bread, the quicker you're dead, I thought. Cornflakes? All starch and where would you find insulin in Laramie, Wyoming at 8:14 A.M. thirty-six feet from the front door of the Antlers Café? I was mumbling all this while the waitress, a short pimply-faced young girl, was waiting.

"I think I'll have an egg," I croaked.

"Goes right to the heart," she said, staring at me and writing nothing down on her pad.

"Oh God," I said. "What'll I do? What can I eat?"

"Well, I tried to stop you last night," said Bert. "You've got nobody to blame but yourself."

I took a wild swing at him but slipped on a piece of bacon on the floor and fell on the table. From there on in, the relationship went downhill. We drove in almost complete silence until Bert asked me the mileage on the speedometer when we passed a wreck so he could write it down for when he would get called as a witness.

Being alone is the second-best thing in the world; the best is being with someone you love. And being alone is the second-worst thing in the world; the worst is being locked in with someone you don't like. That's why the life of good friends and strangers is fine; the business and cocktail life of acquaintanceship is deteriorating.

But this trip became sheer hell. We were trapped in that front seat, Tyrannosaurus Ego and I, and I had to keep holding back my temper, which is the most exhausting thing you can do, and you know it. It's like the opposite of that Strength Through Dynamic Tension pitch that's advertised in all the magazines. Day and night, mile after mile, I had Bert droning on and on and always as though we were a team. He always spoke in the plural.

"Trouble with you and me, Tod," he'd say, "is that we need to be loved too much. That means we seek out people to love us and that can be good for us in our profession. But of course you do fight your own nature and that really will cause you to lose sales. You'd better make calls with me for a couple of weeks and you'll see how to handle all that."

See what I mean? He worked both sides of the street,

a habit I hold in the utmost contempt. First we were alike, then we weren't because he was better. "We're two separate people!" I wanted to say, but I didn't and I didn't discuss it at all with Matilda because she would have blamed me, I knew that. So we just kept driving along, me silent and him practicing how he would make fools of district attorneys and defense lawyers with his vast knowledge of facts on the stand. Matilda took to sleeping in the back seat; then at night, in the motels, which weren't so classy in those days, she'd want to stay up late because she wasn't tired. All in all the trip was awful and all I could see ahead, being in business with this idiot, was a disaster.

God is good. God is merciful. God is Tops in His Field. Because in His Infinite Wisdom He saw fit to make Las Vegas, which got me off the hook. As we approached there, about dusk, Bert got all excited, stimulated. Matilda still slept but even I started to perk up a bit because the sign "Las Vegas 10 Mi." was a symbol of, oh, good times, probably some decent food, surroundings, gaiety. The tank was almost dry, so we pulled into a Chevron station where the attendant, an old man with dried-up face, weather-beaten, but a shock of good brown hair, took care of us.

"Any new hotels we should know about since I was here last?" Bert was as cheerful as a clam.

"Dunno when you was here last."

"Got me there, podner," Bert said.

"Why doncha try El Rancho Vegas?" The old man was spilling gasoline all over the fender while Bert and I waited outside the car for Matilda, who was freshening up in the ladies.

"Great idea!" Bert said. "That's where they have all those Filipino bellboys."

"No, they don't have any Filipino bellboys there at all."

"Well, they used to," said Bert the Undefeated. "One right after the other." He was euphoric.

We got to El Rancho Vegas about five o'clock, checked in, and arranged to meet in the hotel bar at seven-thirty after we napped and showered. Matilda and I went to our room, where I told her I was afraid I was going to kill Bert and she said she'd visit me in the Death Row cell and bring me ciggy-boos and console me in other ways too. Then we did take our nap, showered, etc., and I felt better so we set sail for the bar. Bert wasn't there yet and when I called his room, no answer. We waited about twenty minutes and then went looking for him. The gambling tables were all crowded, and remember at that time I didn't know much about him, but suddenly I heard that voice.

"Come on, you two little deuces! Good ten!! Bring your little brother, the crapshooters in hell saw that one." And so on. I went over to him and he was like a new man: face all flushed, all smiles, and a pile of black chips in front of him. "Those are hundred-dollar chips, pal!" He thrust a pile of them at me. Twenty-five big ones there and he had plenty left in front of him.

"Here, kid, hold these for me, and no matter what I tell you, don't let me have 'em back. Now beat it, go watch the floor show." He smiled.

Matty and I went in, ordered some food, and then Tony Martin came on. While he was singing "When Did You Leave Heaven," Bert came in, sat down, and whispered "Give me that money, kid."

"You told me not to give it to you. Why don't you have a drink and some nice roast beef."

"I don't want roast beef, I want that twenty-five hundred fish now. Give it to me."

"How about a nice salad?"

"Give me that money!" He was whispering so loud

that some people around shushed us.

"But you told me not to give it to you, to hold it."

Bert grabbed my coat collar and shouted, "It's my money, give it to me!"

So I did. Matty and I watched the whole show, then went out to the tables again. There was Bert looking like a man crazed. Tie loose, collar open, and in front of him just a few twenty-five-buck chips and some fives. He looked at me but I know he didn't see me. We went over to a table and waited. I know that look; boozers have it too. Pretty soon he came over. He was tapped out. He tried to put the arm on me for some money, but his heart wasn't in it—he knew this was the moment of truth, when it is Tap City, and he knew I didn't even like him. While we were there one of the pit bosses came over.

"How do you want to take care of this, Mr. L?" he asked, showing a chit which I could see was for three grand.

"I'll be over later," Bert said. "Don't worry, I'm good for it."

Of course the rest is history. He needed money, and you know I didn't want to be in business with him anyway, so I bought the other half of the acreage from him for four grand, and that included the car and all and I left him there. There was no way to tear him out of that joint, dead or alive. I know these fellows too well. Winning isn't an end for them, only losing.

So Matty and I went to bed and the next morning, bright and early left for Lotus Land, the City of Lost Angels.

16

Someone once said that Southern California is the place where you go to bed age thirty and wake up at fifty. The flowers are brighter but they don't smell as good; the strawberries are bigger but don't taste as good. Strange place, strange place. And the time flies right by.

I set us up in a decent furnished apartment on North Sycamore and had to go right to work because we were running short of bread. Matty took to the place like a fish to water. I still can't explain why, but I didn't need to understand it, just accept it and I did. In Las Vegas I'd caught her looking at the little chapel in the hotel where people got married to one another and that had been a matter of some concern to me, another reason why I left so fast, though of course I never told her that. Only would have worried her and I never saw any good reason to hurt another living soul. They may want to hurt you back. What I'm getting at is in L.A. I think Matty thought we were married and let it go at that. I have seen marriages ruin too many good relationships to believe in it, whatever "believing in" means. My friend Alvin Hart, the great horse trainer, had lived with a famous Follies beauty for eleven years when one day, for reasons unknown, they got married. Zip.

Five months later, divorce. I guess it is all choice. When you're living together, you go home because you'd rather. When you're married and think you *have* to go home, it's good-bye Charley and Katy lock the door.

Matty went shopping, changed the apartment around six times in five months, made friends with the neighbors—my God, you'd think she'd been born in a small town instead of in Hell's Kitchen. I got myself all set up with a couple of phones and located a good printer whom Sid the Pearl, a stock nick I knew in New York, had told me about. This guy's name was Svenson and he was a real artist, used the best vellum #8 paper and drew a beautiful design. You've got to understand, these shares of oil leases were the real thing and I wanted my customers to have the best paper. I made my calls, landed some prospects, mostly in the San Fernando Valley, called on them, made some sales. I was selling these leases at $250 a pop, and in the first six weeks I closed on $2,250 which wasn't bad at all in 1946. Of course I still didn't know how well I'd keep going because there was one sale in there to a nice farmer's widow lady in Tarzana of $1,000. And another one to a retired druggist of $500. What I mean is, I only made five sales. But it all looked good.

In the meantime, Matty had made friends with one Lilac L'Orange, a lady who had lilac hair and orange-colored eyebrows and ran a very conservative religious dodge in downtown L.A. called the Alameg Temple. A very smart lady, one of the smartest I've ever known. She was already dabbling in astrology, years ahead of her time, and I heard that a few years ago she gave up the temple entirely and went into astrological soothsaying only, and that now she is investigating becoming a witch. Always moving, Lilac L'Orange, a true leader in her profession.

Also Matty was taking driving lessons, using the Buick when I was contacting my leads on the phone. (You have to make eight and a half phone calls for every invitation to call; and you'll close one sale out of every five meetings. At least I did, and I keep careful records.)

Now let me tell you something about the driving-instruction business.

I got to know some of these driving instructors and they always had you at a disadvantage when they were teaching because they knew things the pupil didn't know, like how to shift, where the brake was, and the like. So being at the wheel was the most important thing in the world at that time; it involved possible death. In short, Fear. When they were teaching women, they went crazy with power. Matilda's instructor was a Herman Wurlitzer, who was never known to be without grease stains on his vest or ever without a vest. He had sandy, thinning hair with plenty of dandruff, gold-frame glasses, hairy ears, round-toed black shoes with brown herringbone suit, filthy. And you must know by now that Matilda was a strong lady who'd been around, street smart, guts of a blind burglar. Yet late one afternoon Matty comes home from a driving lesson with Herman Wurlitzer and announces to me "I'm going to Palm Springs this weekend."

"What the hell are you talking about?"

"Herman says I can drive pretty well around town, but I've got to learn how to drive on the throughways so we're going to drive to Palm Springs on Friday." She was breathless, seemed scared.

"You are not driving to Palm Springs with Herman Wurlitzer. On Friday."

"Do you want him to give me up as a pupil? And I'll never learn to drive? In traffic?" she wailed. I'm sure she had a horrible vision of herself at the wheel on the freeway, telling Herman Wurlitzer she couldn't go to Palm Springs with him, and he calmly walks out the door of the car and there she is alone, with all those levers and wheels.

Anyway, she finally learned to drive around because I taught her and we didn't have to go to Palm Springs at all. I even bought her a nice little Ford all her own and she was happy as a clam because my business was going farther and wider: overnight trips to Fresno and Bakersfield and Modesto and like that. Sales were going pretty good but I was working hard. But then, I've always been a hard worker.

Six years went by. Matilda made a lot of friends at the Alameg Temple and there were some big people in that temple: motion-picture producers, business people and like that. We rented a little house and I put some money into it so Matty could fix it up and entertain the people who had us over from time to time. The social life hadn't changed since I was there before the war. The invitations would always include the menu and cast list.

"Can you come for dinner Friday night? We're having spaghetti with meatballs and Tony Curtis?" they'd ask. Sometimes you'd get the credits, too, if the honored guest wasn't too well known. "She just did the second lead in the new Billy Wilder flick," the hostess would tell you when she handed out the invite on the phone. "We'll just broil some steaks."

I took a run at finding Rip and Dan, but no luck, and somehow I just never ran into the Tradlers, although I heard their name mentioned. They were still married to each other; he'd had a heart attack, she drank. All par for the course and no surprises. But who does show up one day? Father Bob. From good old Rapid City.

One Tuesday night we're home, Matty and I,

watching Milton Berle on TV. Right after his show, there's a local commercial and there's Father Bob, doing a laying on of the hands for some mark, and the old lady he's belting on the chops in order to heal her (he is saying "Heal her, oh Lord! Heal her!") suddenly gets up and does a Charleston, anyway jumps around a lot. Then the announcer says, "The famous Father Bob, who has healed thousands, is appearing one week only at the Los Angeles Philharmonic Auditorium starting Tuesday night, September 29th."

"I knew he'd make the big time," I said to Matty. "I used to know him." And I felt proud, like a baseball scout who had picked Ted Williams in American Legion ball to make the majors. Matty insisted I take her and started almost immediately to complain of arthritic pains in her right shoulder so I also had to take her to dinner at Chasen's the next night since she couldn't handle the skillet. Lilac L'Orange joined us and filled us in over the steaks on Father Bob, whose career she naturally had followed, at least these last few months when he'd started making noises on TV.

"He's been working tents," said Lilac, "and very successful. *Very* successful. I know you don't believe in these things, Tod my dear, but he has healed an awful lot of people."

"I believe in Father Bob more than anyone I've ever known."

"You actually sound fervent," said Matilda while, ignoring the terrible pain in her shoulder that had made me spring for an expensive dinner at Chasen's, she leaned all the way across me to spear half a tomato from my salad plate.

"Well, you may laugh all you want at these things, Tod dear," Lilac said, "and you can deny these miracles happen, that faith is the great healer, or, as Father Bob teaches, that Divine Deliverance is always available to those who are always vulnerable, but I can tell you this: the man made over $2,000,000 last year before taxes."

"But he doesn't take anything for himself," breathed Matilda. "I was reading about him all day."

"The man is a saint," I said. I just wanted to get along and protect my flanks because now Lilac was picking at my potato, too.

"He is a great human being and that's better than a saint," said Lilac Goody Two-shoes. "Because saints are made by humans and humans are made in God's garden."

"Will you keep off my plate, both of you!"

And with that, who do you think walks in? Father Bob, looking gorgeous with the golden hair, a little longer now, all fluffed up. Choppers like a Steinway keyboard. With him was a furtive-looking little woman with small eyes behind a pair of horn-rimmed glasses and two children who looked just like Father Bob. A boy and a girl.

The headwaiter went over to Father Bob and spoke with him, then looked at his list and said something. Father Bob dazzled him with a smile and shook his head; I figured he was told it would be just a few minutes and why didn't he wait at the bar. I don't drink or smoke, I don't need any of that shit was what his smile said. I watched him from behind a forkful of Brizzola steak while the girls attacked my salad and hash browns like two termites working on the Ark. It was a little shaky for me, as though all the years between hadn't passed at all, were wasted, I hadn't grown, learned anything. I looked at the lady with him pretty good too, and she fit what I figured he'd be with: the pursed lips, the hair in a bun under the hat, the sensible shoes, even the glasses. The daughter was about sixteen and the boy, almost as tall, probably about fourteen. The same golden hair, the same look of "Isn't it great to be alive?" to be followed by "Why not try things My Way?" And then they started in together and I saw they were being led by my booth.

17

"Toddy Fleedhurn! I don't believe it."

The children and Missus Father Bob were already gone in the wake of the headwaiter and Father Bob called ahead to them: "You all go on, I'll be right there."

"Father Bob, this is my wife, Matilda Summers." I was so confused that I wanted to tell him she was my wife but not to lie about her name. "And this is Lilac L'Orange."

"Hello, Matilda." He took her hand in both of his, then turned to Lilac. "And of course we have heard of Lilac L'Orange."

"And Lilac knows of you," she said. "Why don't you sit down for a bit?"

"Just for a moment. My lovely family is ravenous."

"We are going to your healing festival, Father Bob," breathed Matty, "on the twenty-ninth."

"I dreamed of you only last night, Toddy," Father Bob said. "We were at a huge feast together." He looked at me and smiled. "So I do hope all three of you will join us that night for supper."

"We'll make your dreams come true, Father Bob," said Matilda.

"Does E.S.P. happen to you a lot?" asked Lilac.

"I have found that since I have completely eschewed all worldly things, all comes to me. Especially the truth. What I feel comes true for I neither want nor need anything from it."

"I see," said Lilac.

"In fact, Toddy"—he turned to me again—"I am getting vibrations from you now. Why don't you come to see me at the Ambassador Hotel on Thursday?"

"I'm going to be in San Jose Thursday."

"I know." He smiled. What a broken-field runner! "And now I must leave you all. See you on the twenty-ninth. We'll have a huge feast."

"Isn't he wonderful," said Matilda. "He doesn't take a penny for himself. Clear and clean and wonderful."

Lilac wasn't listening. She was just watching him go down the aisle.

"That jacket cost at least a hundred and fifty dollars," she said. "Pure cashmere."

Always ask a successful businessman about business, an artist about art, and a temple hustler about temple hustling because they understand one another. Don't go to strangers. Lilac and Father Bob were already closer friends to each other than I could ever be to either.

We had ten days till the big Drop-the-Crutch Festival that Father Bob was throwing. I had a couple of overnight trips I had to make and I invented a couple more; all in all it was the most anxiety-crazed time I've ever been in. I never saw Matty like this. In all the years I had known and lived with her she had never had a sore shoulder or a sore anything else. She always kept doing her dance exercises and was as strong and healthy as a young lioness. Until she read about Father Bob and his curative powers. Since then every day the pain got more unbearable, and finally the day of the

Main Event, she had to carry her arm in a sling, a big black sling.

Lilac was getting panicky too, but in a different way. She was then about fifty—I'm giving her the best of it probably—with leathery skin on the face but a firm little body that was pretty sexy and seemed always thinking about it. I figured that she banged around a lot with her constituents. She was the kind that'd have an orgy with you along with an alligator and a police dog, swinging from the chandeliers and making out with doorknobs and afterwards would say "Excuse me, I have to tinkle." Or "Look, I'm no prude. What the hell, nothing wrong with having a hump with a sheep. But with a goat? That's dirty."

I know she was hot as a two-dollar pistol for Father Bob though she kept getting more silent as the days went by. She and Matty spent hours discussing what to wear. Lilac was into saris then, with her dyed lilac hair and orange eyebrows, and one night I came home and she was trying on a perfectly ordinary suit, going all the other way, but she gave up on that and finally collapsed into one of the deals she wore on her own pulpit. Obviously felt more secure in it.

After several dress rehearsals, Matty was all set to wear her basic black with simple pearls, but she did like that black satin sling, so she settled on a trim little white affair for contrast and a beautiful garnet necklace I'd got her. Good colors, the red, black, and white with her pale skin and black hair which she pulled straight back for the first time since I'd known her. Not unlike Missus Father Bob. Get the picture?

In the midst of all these festivities I got a letter from my mother, who was now living in Chicago, where Preston had moved to when that cough medicine had gone like wildfire in Minnesota and the Pure Food and Drug people had taken a good hard look at it. He'd make a packet so that, she had written me previously, he could take care of the rap and keep out of the slammer but no more cough medicine. As she told me on the phone when all this happened, a couple of years before, when the inspector visited Pres to tell him of the findings, Pres said, "Do you smoke cigars, Inspector?"

"I certainly do," said that worthy.

"What kind of cigars do you smoke?"

"Cadillacs."

So Pres knew where he stood, knew just how to take care of the problem, that is, with a couple of grand, and moved to Chi with what was left of the money, and opened a Bar and Grill.

> **Dear Son of Mine,**
> This is to hereby inform you that your father is dead again. That is, your other father is dead, the step one. Poor Preston is gone to his reward and at the hand of a dumb little shanty Irish Mick maid who he was only good to and who couldn't carry his towel, though she may have, who knows and what difference does it make now?
> You know, I wrote you we bought this old brownstone house to live in and fixed it up. But it had a dumbwaiter. That's a little wooden platform that rides up and down on a rope and a pulley between the kitchen in the basement and all the floors. You buzz downstairs, then tell the kitchen people on an old-fashioned intercom system what you want, and they put it on the dumbwaiter, hoist it up, you open the door which is built in the wall and take it off. Well, we had this new maid who we got and were going to train because she was in the country illegally and we didn't have to pay her hardly anything and were training her so she could have a good decent profession. She was only with us four days when the tragedy occurred.

Poor Preston buzzed and buzzed and buzzed and she didn't know what the hell to do, how to press the right button to answer him. So he opened the dumbwaiter door and leaned in and simply hollered downstairs "You stupid Irish slut, send that dumbwaiter up with a couple of beers!!" That's really the only kind of language they understand, son.

The girl must have panicked because she yanked hard on the ropes and the dumbwaiter, which had been at the floor above, came whacking down with all its might, and hit him on the back of the head.

It doesn't seem right, him having such a hard life all the time and trying to provide pleasure for one and all against all kinds of odds, the govt. and all. And now this. As if living isn't tough enough, but you got to die too. I'll never, never understand it. At least it happened suddenly. He didn't suffer at all. Just your mother suffered.

He didn't leave me too well provided for. I have the house including the dumbwaiter and a few dollars from Social Security. But above all, please don't worry about me. I'll always be able to get some food at the drugstore downstairs where Seymour the counterman and Emory the pharmacist have both become good friends to me.

I have written your brother Jack about all this but have heard nothing from him yet. Of course I only mailed the letter this morning so it wouldn't be fair to expect anything and if there is one thing your mother knows she is at least, it's fair.

Your last letter to me seemed a little sad, son. Are you having problems? Would you like your mother to come there for a visit? My goodness it has been so many years and I would like to meet Martha. The pictures you sent me of her last remind me so much of myself ten years ago. Don't you think it's about time my baby made me a grandmother?

Warmest personal regards,
Your adoring Mother

P.S. I received a long-distance phone call from the loveliest man, that is a man with the warmest most humane voice I have ever heard, who was trying to find you. He had found Jackie in Rapid City, who gave him my number and I gave him your address. He said he was a good friend of yours, a Mr. Bert Larrabee.

I wrote back at once saying we were contemplating a six-month trip to Tahiti and then sat down to give that idea serious consideration. Once again I could feel my life closing in on me. I could handle the regular letters from my mother, who usually told me what to do, because I always kept a minimum of a thousand miles between us at all times. But Father Bob and Bert Larrabee showing up at the same time! Two positive thinkers. Holy smoke. And of course living with, by now, not only Matty but also Lilac L'Orange, who had moved into an apartment right next door to our little house, had numbed me. I simply always did what they wanted, went where they wanted me to go. I had learned early to compromise with others but now I was compromising with myself.

I waited for the call from Bert Larrabee, dreading it yet anxious to get it. To get it over with? I don't know. I do know that what is real is always deeper, more awful, more sweet than what you imagine. Sure enough, three days later, two days before Father Bob's jamboree, the phone rang on a Saturday night during the "Show of Shows." When I talk with someone whose name I don't remember or whom I don't like, I get terribly effusive. I used to run into people in New York or Hollywood whose name I couldn't get in my mind and I think that's terribly insulting so I'd always say "How are you, darling? Can I buy you a drink? Lunch, a car, something?" Awful. I'd recognize them but wouldn't know who they were. Know what I mean? I do not do that any more. I still don't remember their names but I don't give a damn. Let them remember mine now.

Larrabee has never identified himself on the phone. He was one of those people who'd just start talking and then if you had to say "Who is this?" he'd be hurt. Set himself up to be hurt, the son of a bitch. He *never* said who it was on the phone. When I think of it now I boil.

"Hello," I answered after the third ring, carefully.

"Tod, you old rascal! How would you like me and the little lady of my choice to buy dinner for you and Matilda?"

"Sounds great." I honestly wasn't sure who it was. "Who's this?"

Pause.

"Why, it's Bert Larrabee." Cold.

"Gee, how the heck are you, Bert? Haven't seen you in too many years." That warmed up the son of a bitch.

"When you talk like that I could listen to you all day, Tod. Too many years. Good pals should see each other a lot more often than we have. Now what about that dinner? Can you make it tonight? My wife's dying to meet you both."

"Hell, you both come over here for dinner." All my life I have been a patsy for guys offering me things, trying to buy the first drink, or whatever. I always insist "No, no, let me" and of course Bert accepted the invite. I told Matty they were coming over and she looked at me like I was crazy.

"I thought you didn't like him."

"That was a long time ago." I felt uncomfortable. "And, he did give me that list that we've been living on for years, remember."

"You bought the list, Tod. With the money you earned the hard way, getting shot at in France. Also you used that list up a long time ago. And why do we have to have people for dinner when I can't move my arm and it's only two days till Father Bob's Meet with God and I'm nervous as a cat."

"Well, that's really it. I thought it would get your mind off your pain. We can get Lupe to help us, with the cooking and everything." Lupe was a wetback who did part time for us.

"I'll never understand you, Tod. I'll just never understand you."

Who asked her to?

18

Bert and his wife, Godiva, showed up a half hour late at seven-thirty. She told us later that her real name was Ellen but she'd used the other handle as an exotic dancer, liked it, and kept it. Bert had even had her change the name legally, which was a surprise since that's about the only thing he ever did legally and was the one thing no one would have blown a whistle on anyway. She probably did a little hooking in the past, too, before she met him and he wanted to wipe the slate clean. Men are funny that way sometimes. Big, brassy blonde, just what you'd expect. A little heavy now, but still attractive and Bert was obviously real proud of her.

Bert had changed a bit. Lost most of his hair, what was left he sleeked back, and had acquired a bit of paunch in the time we'd been apart. But he was well dressed, as always, and seemed pretty much at ease so I figured he'd been doing O.K. It developed that he'd been hustling eyeglasses, of all things.

"I graduated and got a diploma from a real distinguished school: the Jefferson Academy of Optometry."

"Terrific, Bert, I really admire someone who goes back to school at your age. Where is it?"

"It's a correspondence school and, in most people's opinion, the best. It's a six months' course and cost a lot of money, but I worked my way through with the Bible Dodge. All through southern Illinois and upper Kentucky. Incidentally, Tod, that's a good business for you, especially now with Korea and all; you know, get war lists, deliver a Bible to the mother or widow, well really the mothers; the widows don't go for a dime, they're too pissed off at the guy for getting killed."

"I know the deal." I felt uncomfortable because somehow I never liked that action. Maybe because I'd been overseas and Bert had never even been shot at. He did bring out the worst in me. I mean I know we all have to do what we can to make a buck and not get caught and all that and here I was thinking this racket was no good when I knew any number of connies who'd made a good decent living at it.

"It's good money, Toddy, and you could use it in towns you're working with something else. You can make $300 a week at it easy: no sweat."

"I don't want to do it, that's all."

"Sometimes we're very self-destructive, aren't we?" Bert said. "Don't you agree, Matilda?"

"If you're speaking of Toddy, I think he's marvelous," she said. I looked at her. What she said made me feel terrific. Then she turned to Bert's wife. "How long have you all been in Hollywood, Godiva?"

"Why, just six months, that's all?" She had that Southern way of ending statements with a question mark. I found out she was actually from Milwaukee, but she'd worked around Louisiana and Arkansas a lot and hung around with musicians because of her act, and most of them like to talk Southern when they can. "And I think it's absolutely scrumptious?"

"Yes, the weather is glorious."

"Oh, deedy-doo yes. But the people are so darned

funny. I mean strange funny, not funny funny, aren't they?"

"Now, dear," said Bert, "people are people every-where."

"Oh, of course, of course," then she sort of giggled to herself. "But they seem to have different values? And I just have to get used to it?"

"What do you mean?" asked Matty, honest as the day is long.

"Well, f'rinstance just last Tuesday I was walking down Rodeo Drive in Beverly Hills, near Wilshire, and I stopped for a light, waitin' to cross, when I noticed someone standin' next to me and Lordy me, it was Cary Grant and he said . . . no, wait a minute, I'm tellin' a lie. It was Wednesday, because Tuesday I went to the dentist for root-canal work on a bicuspid."

"What'd he say, what'd he say?" asked Matty.

"Oh. He said 'I'd like to tear your clothes off and kiss you all over.' Well, I tell you, I was *amazed,* I mean Cary Grant and all. But before I could do anything, the light changed . . . no I *was* right, it was *Tuesday,* after all. Anyway the light changed, like I said, and he ran across the street."

"My God," said Matty, "I've lived out here years and the only movie star I have seen is Lillian Gish. And Cary Grant said he wanted to tear off your clothes? And do what?"

"Or was it Wednesday?" Godiva murmured. "I'm such a scatterbrain."

Bert beamed through the whole outrageous thing. So through the evening we got one or two more including things about how po' li'l her had changed the nation by being at a party in Washington with "Supreme Court Justices? Know what Ah mean? And standing around with a couple of them, while they were holding cocktails and discussing some law that Congress was proposin' and Ah didn't just want to stand there with mah bare face hangin' out, and Ah had read something about this so Ah said 'Well, wouldn't that have to be excluded on account of the Eighth Amendment?' and one of them, why he almost spilled his drink—I believe it was that cute Justice Douglas—he said, 'By George, I believe she's right. We'd better tell Harry' and they walked off to this little fellow playing the piano on the other side of the room, and, well, it is the law of the land now. And Ah was just makin' conversation. Know what Ah mean?"

"She's a pistol," said Bert. "Brightest girl I ever met, present company excepted, of course, Matilda. Reads all the time."

"I have a mind and I like to use it," she said primly. "Just like my body." Here she and Bert burst into gales of laughter and she gave him a shot in the ribs with her elbow. "Know what Ah mean?"

After a few Margaritas, things really got going even for me, and then Lupe served us the #3 Plate of Pork Enchiladas, Cheese Tacos, Tamales, and Heartburn. While Godiva was regaling Matty with more stories of all the movie stars and even civilians who wanted to rip all the clothes off her innocent body, Bert told me how he had opened optometry concessions in stores around the Northwest; Idaho, Washington, and Oregon, and also done a farm-to-farm eyeglasses business wrapping up whole families at a time, until he had tried to put a contact lens on some cowboy's glass eye and had got run out of Pocatello. He'd been reported and it developed that the authorities in Idaho took a dim view of correspondence-school graduates in the optometry field; to put it another way, they didn't accept them and they blew the whistle on him in other states. So he'd come down here, pushing Bibles on the way.

"We might just settle here," said Bert. "I've worked hard for a long time. How old do you think I am?"

"About forty-eight," I lied.

"Fifty-seven. I know I look younger because I take care of my body and my body takes care of me. And I've always eaten the right foods. Anyway, we have accumulated a little money, actually more than a little; that was a good score up there while it lasted. I've got very close to a quarter of a million." He looked for my admiration and he got it. Matilda found out later from Godiva that she had been married previously to an Arkansas pork farmer who had died quite suddenly and left her $300,000, which accounted for Bert's bundle and relieved my feeling of failure.

He carried on some more with me because the two ladies were in another corner dishing like they'd known each other for thirty years and he said again he thought he'd buy a house out in the San Fernando Valley and settle down.

"I could never really retire," he said. "I've been too active all my life. Godiva and I have been talking about opening a small strip club here, nothing sensational. In fact I looked at a joint today on Santa Monica Boulevard that might be right for us."

"We wouldn't need stars," Godiva said. "I could take some new kids and teach them. Then they would have a profession."

"We would be performing a needed service," Bert said, "which I am happy to do. This joint is a restaurant and gypsy fortunetelling store that Lefty Fenner is running. You remember him, don't you?"

"From Philly? Sure."

"Well, he's going down to Mexico and I can buy the whole magillah, the restaurant and an astrological-chart mag with a pretty good subscriber list. You know, 'This is a good time for you to be alone;

however, you will need your friends more than ever' or 'You must learn to be less unselfish.' So that would give me a chance to be creative, which, let's face it, I must be or I can't be happy."

"Bertie is miserable when he isn't creating."

"So with the strip joint and the star suckers, we might make a good life, eh, Poopsie?" He patted her ass as she walked over to sit with Matty.

"I sure wish you all the luck in the world, Bert."

"I know that, kid," he said, clapping me on the back. I felt I was suddenly going crazy, saying things I didn't mean and all that. Of course, you don't go crazy suddenly. I poured myself a huge Scotch and one for Bert.

Meanwhile the girls over in the corner were talking and laughing and Godiva let out a whoop.

"You don't really," she said.

"We do too," said Matilda.

"Bert, they know Father Bob," Godiva called over. "And they're going to the revival meeting on Thursday. Let's us go too."

"We'll never be able to get tickets," he said.

"We can get them for you. My Toddy knows Father Bob real well," Matilda said proudly. After all the things I had done for her, the fact that I knew a great man was what impressed her. Then I thought, Who says he's a great man? Just because his name was all over the newspapers and billboards. I took another depressed drink.

"Do you really, kid?" Bert asked. "You've come a long way since I saw you last."

"I knew Father Bob before I ever met you."

"Can you really get us tickets? I heard from a guy I know who knows Harry Marx, who books the auditorium, that they never had to make a deal like the one they had to make to get Father Bob. The circus, fights, all the other events leave the place a chance to make some money of their own. But he takes it all: tickets, programs, pictures, popcorn, all the concessions. And he's been sold out for days. You won't be able to get us tickets."

"Oh?" I said. "Let's see about that." I thought savagely, I'll get those damn tickets; nobody tells me what I can or can't do. And the next day I got two more tickets after five phone calls to Father Bob's secretary and manager and who-all. Then I thought, I didn't even want them to go with us. What was I doing? Those days I was always rooting for a horse I didn't bet on. Bad habit. Awful bad habit.

So we went. Lilac, Godiva, Bert, Matilda, and me. Sure enough there were five tickets waiting for us at the box office at only ten bucks a crack but right in row double A. And what a crowd milling in. Folks from every walk of life and some who could hardly walk at all, on crutches, in wheelchairs, leaning on one another. I take the position that the great preponderance of them were legit though of course he had some timber there in case of a tie. I did see Terry McCormack, who sometimes worked as a stick for the Ocean Park Pokerino game, and he was heavy on crutches although if a cop were chasing him he'd have as much of a limp as Charley Paddock in his prime.

As the people filed in, we all got a feeling of respect, bordering on reverence then awe, as oh so slightly one became aware of the organ music piping in, over several speakers throughout the auditorium. The lighting was muted, and when almost all the audience had filed in, the choir sneaked on stage, stood silently for a moment, then went into its first hymn. The boys all had freshly scrubbed faces with crew cuts and the girls had long hair, mostly blond. There were two black faces, one boy and one girl; Father Bob was always ahead of his time, but not so far ahead as to get into trouble. They did a couple of numbers, the first soft and then a good rocking hymn, and then they cut that abruptly off at the end and just stood there. The lights dimmed, the place was dark for only a moment, long enough to strike that instant of expected fear and suddenly . . .

The beam of the spotlight picked up Father Bob, high on a pedestal, looking up to You Know Who, then down to all of us. His hair shone and so did his teeth as he smiled and when he did you could hear 18,000 people exhale in relief. He was All-Powerful but he hadn't killed them. Yet.

"I come to you humbly and am grateful to you for receiving me."

"Oh, thank you, Father Bob," someone shouted.

Then he went into his pitch, which wasn't too much unlike what he was using when I first heard him thirty years before, just expanded a lot. The same business of chastising them because they were sinners because they weren't using themselves properly. "Truth" and "Love" were very highly spoken of. "There is a Truth of the moment and an accumulative Truth," he said and that got 'em where they lived, in positive ignorance.

He got that crowd and, I've got to tell you the truth, he got me, too. He had me, I believed him. I looked over to Bert and tears were streaming down his cheeks as folks walked with crutches or limped or were wheeled to the podium to be healed. Godiva kept falling to her knees and yelling "Praise, oh Praise!!" and my Matilda joined the parade after it had started going a little. The only one who knew what the hell was really going on was Lilac, who would shake her head from time to time in admiration but who always obeyed when called on, knelt, prayed, whatever he said. Real professional courtesy. He kept healing them a mile a minute, at least most of them. There was one young fellow, about nineteen, who was brought to the podium by his mother who said the kid was deaf. I thought he might be a shill but as Father Bob was clenching the kid's head and shouting "Oh heal this man, Lord, make him hear, make him hear," the kid kept saying "What'd he say? What'd he say?" till the old lady rapped him hard across the shoulder and led him back to his seat so that now the kid was not only deaf but also had a sore shoulder and was disappointed in himself, felt he had failed God *and* his mother. However, Father Bob had a stick come up next, Terry McCormack, who dropped his crutches on cue, so that everything still looked good and the tip didn't lose its confidence in the healer.

Soon Matilda got up there. She was looking at him with eyes that I had never seen on her before. She was ready to do anything for him. So when he put both hands on her head, closed his eyes and said "Heal her, heal her, oh Lord!" and then ordered her, "Throw away that sling!" she did and, since she was truly a theatrical person, she winged it across the stage like a second baseman on a double play. Then she did the whole bit; this woman who hadn't been able to mash a potato for two weeks, she flung her arms up in the air and praised the hell out of the Lord. Then she came back to me and gave me the hottest wettest kiss ever.

Finally the spotlight went out on Father Bob, the choir hummed him off, and the house lights went up. We waited for Father Bob. The crowd which was quite ruly filed out the back of the auditorium and then we found a stage door guarded by what looked like an old heavyweight, but Father Bob, who was nothing if not organized, had left word for us and we went to his dressing room where there were already a couple of dozen fans including the deaf kid and his mother, who was talking to Father Bob when we entered. I must say Father Bob earned his keep because he was seated, obviously exhausted, and sweated up like a horse after going a mile and three sixteenths. But he still smiled as he held one of the boy's hands in both of his and looked at the kid's face while the mother rattled on. The poor kid was pretty, almost with the look of a girl, though he had plenty of pimples. Only one of them was suppurating that I could see and in Father Bob's look I could see love. I don't mean the Fellowship-of-Man-Under-Eternal-God love, I mean the Real Thing, let's-get-our-ashes-hauled love for this boy.

"He's a good boy, Father Bob; it's just that he won't hear and it's all that I can bear sometimes," the mother whined on. "He does have a job at the Owl Drug Store at the counter, where he makes the Take Out sandwich orders, while the other countermen give him written orders. Well," etc., she droned on.

"Is this the face that shipped a thousand lunches?" I heard Father Bob say softly with love. Then he kissed the kid sweetly on the lips and said to the mother, "He shall hear."

She fell to her knees, got up, and led the poor bewildered deaf kid out of there, muttering to him, "Now if you don't hear, it will be your fault. I've done everything any mother can do and even Father Bob . . ."

Matty pushed her way up, along with Lilac, and grabbed one hand while she tearfully looked at him. He smiled graciously at her but exchanged a different kind of look with Lilac.

"You healed me, Father Bob. I never thought I could move that arm again."

"It was Jesus who did it, daughter."

"Then I thank Jesus." She was most fervent.

"I am just the one who lays on his hands to make His healings happen."

"I do thank you too, Father Bob."

"It went real good, Father Bob," I heard Lilac say to him in an undertone.

"I thought the opening was slow, but after a couple of healings it went all right, smooth as cream," he said. Then I got there and we shook hands. He squeezed my hand a little. For years, when other men had done that, I thought they were a little queer, till I found out that it was the Masons' grip. With Father Bob I didn't know what the hell it was because he was a Mason too.

"It was wonderful," I said. "Moving as well as most impressive."

"I'm glad you think so. You're the one I wanted to please, Toddy." Then he turned to a heavyset man who was standing nearby smoking a big cigar and sweating slightly while listening to another man whose lips barely moved. This second fellow was about a head shorter than the big man, was beautifully sun-tanned, and had gorgeous wavy gray hair. Father Bob spoke to the big man. "This is Mr. Placer; Emmett, shake hands with one of my oldest friends, Toddy Fleedhurn."

Well, I knew who Mr. Emmett Placer was. His late father had invented some kind of valve without which your internal-combustion engine just won't run, it might as well be a kiddie car, so every time one of those engines is built, Emmett gets $3.84. He was one of the richest men in the United States and I was mightily impressed to meet him. He in turn introduced me to the other gent, Dr. Ernst Shilto.

Father Bob's wife, whom I hadn't met yet, came in with another lady who I was introduced to later as Mrs. Emmett Placer and with a quite young girl—actually I made her about fourteen then but later she said she was eighteen. She said. She was a member of the choir and was named Purita Somerville, from Baton Rouge, Louisiana. Purita was an odd name for her because that is a kind of spic monicker, with that "a" on the end, whereas she was as blonde as you can be, with fair skin, peaches-and-cream complexion, we used to say.

Father Bob went behind a screen to change his clothing while his wife—"My name is Imogene but please call me Gene"—told us that the two children had gone back to Fort Worth, where they now lived, for the start of school. Mrs. Emmett Placer never spoke a word, just stood there and looked dazzlingly pleasant with her beautifully coiffed hair, sparkling teeth, translucent skin, and with her tailored satin slacks that showed her ass that you could eat off. Mr. Emmett Placer knew what to do with his money. As I say, she just stood there, which was enough. And it wasn't till later that I found she was stoned out of her mind on cocaine. She never said one word till Father Bob came out dressed in a custom-made gray sharkskin suit and turned-around collar and said, "We're all going up to the house where Gene's laid on a beautiful supper and we can really get to know each other."

"I've got to go along with that kind of thinking," she said and then she giggled. I never found out her real name, which is surprising when you think of all that happened later, but everyone called her Bubbles.

There were three limousines with drivers waiting at the stage door, plenty of room for all, but I never like to be stranded without my own car in California, so we let Matilda, Lilac, and Godiva go with the others, which I knew they wanted to do, and Bert drove with me in my car after we got directions, which were tricky, to Emmett's house where Father Bob and Gene were staying.

I drove the car while Bert, who had carefully listened

to the directions, sat next to me and navigated. He still behaved as though someone very important was watching everything he did and was going to ask him questions about it all. The only time I'd ever seen him break out of this witness box was when he was shooting craps at Vegas. I remembered listening to the directions too, and when we got to a fork in the road, I started going to the left.

"No, we go to the right here, kid," he said. "I wrote it all down."

"I'm sure it's to the left." I pulled over to the side.

"It's to the right. You know you have no sense of direction. Now I'm positive."

We went to the right and wound up on top of a mountain in Hollywood with absolutely nothing but rocks and trees around us.

"You dumb son of a bitch," I yelled. "I told you we should go to the left.

"You had the wheel," he said calmly. How do you like that? I really hated that man. If you had told me then that an hour later I'd be in bed with him, I'd have called you a liar.

Finally, after retracing our steps and getting lost again, I insisted on going along with what I remembered rather than Bert's notes and we got to a huge iron gate near Mulholland Drive high above Hollywood. By now it was raining pretty hard and we had to wait for the guard at the gate to get into his black raincoat, get our names, and call up to the house. Then he unlocked the gate and we drove up a long winding driveway, getting glimpses of the huge mansion from time to time on turns, till we arrived at the front door. I rang the bell and was surprised that the door was opened by Emmett Placer himself. There were no servants there that night at all, at least I never saw any.

"What the hell happened to you guys?" Emmett asked.

"He got us lost." I pointed to Bert.

Emmett led us through the foyer and a tremendous living room furnished in modern Chinese Ugly into a den where all the others were sitting around. There was a buffet laid on with lots of cold cuts and a couple of chafing dishes and there was an odd odor around that I couldn't or didn't identify at first but you know what it was and then when I saw Gene, Father Bob's wife, puffing on a funny-looking cigarette, I remembered back when Matilda used to have those musicians and Communists around the house all the time, before the war, and they'd drag pot. They called it muggles then. Nobody was eating yet or even had a plate of food except Purita, who was sitting at Gene's feet and nibbling at some stuff on her plate. From time to time Gene would lean down and put some more food in the kid's mouth, like she was her daughter or something.

We must have broken up some kind of serious conversation, because as soon as we came in they all went to the groaning board and got food. There was a bar set up at one end of the table but the only one who was drinking any booze was Emmett Placer himself, who never stopped, all night, pouring himself great tumblers of bourbon whiskey with just a little branch water. Everybody else was getting high on some other stuff, if only ideas.

Now you have to understand that I was petrified with anxiety right then. I felt—hell, we all felt—that we were in the presence of greatness in the person of Emmett Placer. He had what we all wanted, money; he'd gotten it easily and a lot of it too, maybe a quarter of a billion's worth, without sweating a drop. So he must have been smart or something, and if he wasn't, he could buy smarts. Any of ours, for sure. And let me tell you about money.When you run into an old school chum and say "How's Tom?" and he says "Tom's doing very well" that means one thing: money. Tom may not be doing anything well. "How's Fred?" "Fred's very successful." Image? Two cars, and swimming pool.

So let me tell you, even those of us who were hanging on to others a step above, even those of us, including Mrs. Father Bob and Bubbles, who were holding on to the trapeze dangling from the feet of Dr.

Ernst Shilto, were halfway up old Emmett Placer's ass. So there we were, all trying to impress this big tub. And he knew it, that's what I respected most about him. He knew it and he liked it and he knew how to accept it and he wouldn't have accepted anything less. I learned a lot from that man.

"Talked to my broker today," Emmett said, his little eyes twinkling behind the rimless glasses. Did I tell you he wore a vest? Well, he did and now, though his jacket was off, he still had his vest on with an old-fashioned chain going across, Elks' tooth and all. "I asked how we were doing. Old broker, he said 'The market's firming down to a nice base' and I said 'You mean I'm getting wiped out and you're trying to break it to me nice and easy.'" He laughed merrily. "They have more ways of giving bad news than a cat has kittens."

"I hope you weren't too worried," I said.

"No," he answered, seriously. "If I learned one thing in the little game called ell eye eff ee, it's that money isn't all that important."

"Money isn't all that important?" I almost screamed.

"No, hear me out. The lack of it is terrible, I suppose, but having it doesn't mean a thing. It's what I call 'a paradox.'" He said that as though the word had no real existence till he spoke it.

"That is very good, Emmett," said Dr. Ernst Shilto.

"Thank you," Emmett said humbly.

"I'd believe that more if I heard it from someone who didn't have a couple of hundred million dollars," I said. But Father Bob broke in, to save my ass.

"Why don't we try that arrangement Ernst was talking about last night. Might serve us all well," he said. "As indeed, we all must serve." You can take the boy out of the pulpit but you can't take the pulpit out of the boy.

"I do not know if we are all ready for it," said Shilto with his slight German accent. I found out later that he was actually Bavarian, whatever that means. And then he went on to explain what some of them had heard before, how we all are covered up by too many things mostly from our environments. Cultural pressures, family influences, economics, and how we had to get down to the core, take some chemical help and touch one another. Simple.

While the doctor was talking Father Bob must have slipped out because the next time I noticed him he was standing in the doorway dressed only in a bright-orange jockstrap. He waited till everyone saw him and then he took that off. I was amazed, though perhaps I shouldn't have been, remembering him from Rapid City and his grabs at my very own jewelry. Dr. Ernst Shilto nodded and said "Very good, Father Bob." Nobody else said or did anything.

"But we must do more," said Shilto thoughtfully, removing his own jacket and loosening his tie. "We must always do more. For we must the leaders be."

So it all began to hit the fan. Soon we were all naked as jaybirds except Emmett Placer, who was chortling as though he were watching his children at play.

"The heart of me touches the heart of you," Shilto declaimed solemnly as he embraced good old Lilac L'Orange. She dug immediately that this was an organized deal so she turned around and embraced my Matilda.

"The heart of me touches the heart of you," she said.

So it went. I was shocked but tried to arrange it so that I could touch the heart of Purita by pushing near her when it was her turn but I got a shot in the ribs from Gene's elbow that would have felled an ox if an ox had been dumb enough to be there naked, so I wound up with Bubbles, who must have had some heart to beat through those knockers, but I was timid grabbing her what with her husband chortling right there and yet having enough money to wish me dead if he didn't like the scene. Then the doctor began dropping LSD (I found out later what it was) and grass was being handed around and Father Bob left for a bit to get some cocaine for those who wanted that. I did notice that Shilto didn't partake of any of this and I didn't at all either, but even without it things got dicey for me because the fumes were making me lightheaded. Then I was lying on a great round bed I hadn't even seen before (were we in another room?) with Bubbles on one side of me and Bert Larrabee on the other. Bubbles passed me one of those cigarettes she was smoking and I took a few drags. I remember thinking, I'll compromise with others but never with myself. I want to be a good sport and I want the whole world (which for me was there then) to like me so I'll smoke but I won't like it. Would I behave the same way at a lynching? I couldn't answer that. I gave what was left of the cigarette to Bert, who took one puff, and then Father Bob appeared.

"Excuse me," he said. Bert got up and gave Father Bob his place. Father Bob started right in playing with the old jewelry again, thirty years later, my God what stick-to-it-iveness, while Bubbles was kissing me and flinging her casabas all over me. I had no energy to resist but nothing was happening with my dong. Dr. Ernst Shilto came over to watch the proceedings.

"No erection, eh?"

"Absolutely none, Doctor," said Father Bob.

"Glub, glub," said Bubbles Placer.

"I vunder vy," said the doctor thoughtfully.

"Well, you're standing there staring at me, for a start, that's why," I shouted.

"That may be ze reason. Ve cannot rule out any possibility. But zere must be a reason. Zere is always a reason."

I finally got up enough initiative to push Father Bob away. He stood up, looking hurt, but thoughtful, already planning his next move. Shilto sat on the edge of the bed where Father Bob had been.

"Ve can always find out vy things do not happen. Though never vy they do. Grass vill not grow through rock because ze rock is too hard."

"That could never be said of you, buster," said Bubbles, stopping her work for a moment. Then she added as she leaped forward again to start, "Buster darling."

"But vy does grass grow at all? Vot is a seed?" Dr. Shilto was idly fingering my pubic hairs. "Vot is an erection? Ve can know vy they do not happen but never vy they do. Ve are just groping."

That was all too much. I jumped to my feet, happily knocking Dr. Ernst Shilto to the floor, and looked around for Matilda, who might be in jeopardy. The room was pretty dark but I could make out Bert in a corner, still naked, talking to Emmett Placer, who had on his vest, trousers, etc., along with a glass of booze and ice and that curiously gave me confidence. Bert was pitching like mad but whatever he was selling I knew Emmett Placer was not going to buy. You don't inherit millions of dollars by being a dope; I'll bet that Emmett Placer got more free meals from pitchmen without buying any than you've got hair on your head or any place else. I walked over to them to ask where Matty might be and heard just enough of the conversation to find out that I was right. I love to be right.

"It's very conservative, I realize," Bert was saying. "But this kind of deal will give you a good feeling of security."

"I have never had a fiscal anxiety," Emmett said, smiling into his $200,000,000, give or take $50,000,000.

"Where is my Matilda?" I asked.

"Over there, with Father Bob," said Bert, pointing to a dark corner.

"She's in good hands. Don't worry," said Emmett Placer.

Oh how I hate being reassured. How the hell does he know when I should worry? What makes him think I do? Matty was there, smiling, holding both her hands in Father Bob's, and though I was a little stoned I knew that she was pretty far gone and all I wanted to do was get her out of there. I didn't want to gain anything, I was just playing for a tie, but I was playing all out, as hard as I could.

I saw Matty up close there, smiling so believingly at Father Bob, who was still holding her hands, and I knew that whether she knew it right then or not, she needed me and that I loved her. Because love is being needed, it's not needing like so many think. She was so beautiful. Matilda was my definition of beauty. Not to be understood. To be accepted. To be loved. And all my love welled up in me. I had to express my love.

"What the goddam hell are you doing over here, you stupid bitch?" I asked. She kept smiling beatifically as Lilac L'Orange, whom I had just noticed, was sitting with her hand on Matty's thigh while watching over it all was good old naked Father Bob. "We've got to go home," I said.

"She is home, Toddy," said Father Bob. "She is in God's house."

Every sin is committed, every war is waged, in the name of God or Love or Truth. Parents beat their children because they "love them." One guy will tell another, "I saw your wife go into the Bide-a-wee Motel with your best friend. I just had to tell you the truth. No matter how hard it was for me."

If Father Bob wants to tell his flock "God is tops in his field. When they made God, they broke the mold," it's fine with me. But now he was invading my Matilda, and that was personal. I had to take care of that. I believe in personal vengeance, because I can feel it. Someone hurts someone I love, I want to hurt that person. Anyone with a kid knows all that. What I'm against is group vengeance. Everybody getting together for a lynching, and all that. No, this was just me and Father Bob. I grabbed Matilda and pulled her towards me even while her eyes were still on him.

"Come on," I yelled, "put some clothes on, for God's sake."

I would have thought, since all these people were doped up on one thing or another, that no one would pay any mind to the yelling. But I have thought a lot of things that weren't and aren't so and I suppose that comes of being an absolutist. I knew that then but I didn't realize it. I was still living that allegorical life I learned from the white hats and the black hats at Penelope Ann Partridge's Tivoli Gardens Movie Palace with William S. "Bill" Hart and Tom Mix and John Miljan and all those. I know, I do know, that all life is a matter of degree: there is an iodine dose to kill you and one to cure you. But what the hell is the magic-degree number?

From all the dark corners of the room came the others, slowly, disengaging themselves from each other, over to see what was happening.

"The heart of me touches the heart of you." Gene, Father Bob's wife, grabbed me with both hands on my ass.

"For Christ's sake, stop saying that!" I cried and then saw Purita. I felt I had heapened myself by hollering so I took this Purita, this bit of fluff, in my own two arms and said, "The heart of me touches the heart of you, honey."

"Ve never use ze names, any names. Zat is wrong," said Dr. Shilto.

"You see, Fleedhurn . . ." Emmett Placer started to say.

"No names!" shouted Shilto.

"Sorry." Placer couldn't have been pleasanter. "The doctor has explained that intimacy has no nomenclature, it is from God."

"From God," Father Bob repeated.

"For instance," Placer went on, "if I place my hand on this breast, it mattereth not whosoever's breast it is . . ." With that he put his big paw on Matilda's breast and with *that* I hit him right on the jaw and he fell over a chair. Wonderful. Beautiful. See what I mean about personal vengeance? And calling things by their right names? And hitting at the one you are angry at?

Lots of blood, lots of shouting. I took Matty into the next room where our clothes were, had to help her get dressed because she was still stoned, and put my own clothes on. Bert Larrabee came into the room. He was in real good shape, too good shape. I realized, knowing Bert, that he had probably faked smoking pot or drinking or anything because in Placer he had smelled, he thought, the Main Chance which was heady enough for him. He was still naked when he came in, and plenty mad.

"Do you realize what you've done?" His face was

close to mine, and very white. "We've blown one of the greatest marks it has been our lot to come in contact with. That man is worth a quarter of a billion dollars. Just one per cent of that invested carefully in eight-per-cent bonds would be enough to keep both of us in clover for the rest of our lives."

"We didn't do anything, Bert baby," I said. I was finished dressing Matilda and putting my own pants on. "*I* did it and I have never been gladder of anything. And now if you don't get out of my way, I'm going to belt you too."

Bert's glare suddenly turned admiring. He put his big arms around me.

"The heart of me touches the heart of you," he said.

"Oh, hell," I said, embracing him. "The heart of me touches the heart of you too."

The next day Matilda didn't wake up till three o'clock in the afternoon. She was always a late sleeper but not like this and I was beginning to worry until she did come to, with a great big headache, but alive. And very quiet. It was almost an hour before she could talk, except to ask for some milk for her cereal and say "Thank you."

"I don't really remember what happened last night."

"That's all right, honey," I said.

"I mean, I remember a whole lot of dreams and things, Toddy, but I can't tell which were the dreams."

"Well, we fell in with evil companions." She was weeping a little bit now so I wiped her eyes. Then in walked Lilac L'Orange.

"Right after you left, we all got dressed and went home too. Are you O.K., Matty?"

"I'm fine."

"Mr. Emmett Placer is going to have one sore jaw today, Tod. I'm not sure you didn't make a big mistake, hitting him."

"My Tod didn't make any mistakes," Matty said. "He hit that son of a bitch right on the button."

"And if I did, it's all right with me," I told Lilac,

whom I didn't like at all and this morning the feeling was getting deeper.

"My God, I had a fantastic dream," said Matty, squinting her eyes.

"What was it, dearie? Let's hear it." Lilac tried to get cozy with Matty, who just looked at her as if she were noticing her for the first time.

"I'd rather tell Tod alone."

"Oh. I can take a hint."

"That wasn't a hint," said Matty. "It was a suggestion."

Lilac left without saying a word.

"I shouldn't have done everything I did last night, Tod, I just shouldn't have."

"Oh honey, we all got way out of line. I shouldn't have brought you there."

"No, Tod. I am responsible for what I do. My dream showed me that, maybe it did; anyway I know it. The fact that I know I am responsible, personally, for my own actions means I am free. I always wanted to get my own way and have someone else—you these last years—pay the freight. But only if I'm my own woman can I be some man's woman, I know that now. I made a mistake last night and I am responsible."

"Oh Matty, you shouldn't feel so guilty."

Matilda looked surprised.

"I don't feel guilty. I said I feel responsible. But you've got to hear my dream, because it's all your fault."

MATILDA'S DREAM

We were in some sort of room, New York room, fairly dark and barely furnished at all. You were in the corner with four or five other men, all men, playing cards and the table was completely empty, it didn't even have any cards on it or anything. In fact, as I think of it now you all were holding your hands as though they had playing cards in them, but I didn't see any cards, maybe there weren't any. Your hands were empty, yes I'm sure of that now. The table was plain dull dark wood and you were on chairs, straightback chairs. I couldn't tell you now who those other men were if my life depended on it. And my life doesn't depend on it.

I was standing center stage, down front. Did I tell you this was a play and we were on stage? Well, we were. And I was brightly illuminated and holding my baby to my breast, nursing it. Didn't I tell you I had a baby? What a beautiful child!

Then a man comes out from stage left, the other side from where you all are playing cards, dressed in a black cloak and hood with his face hidden. The point is that I was also a spectator, part of the audience, and I gasped as I saw him, but as the woman on stage, the one I really am, I didn't know he was there at all. I was much too busy feeding my baby and burping my baby and holding my baby and cooing to my baby. SO ALL THROUGH THE REST OF IT, UP TO THE END, I NEVER EVEN KNEW HE WAS THERE.

Then he says to me, "I have come for you," and here he looked into the folds of his cloak where his right hand would be, as if checking his list, "Matilda Jo Summers." Very solemn. Then a moment later he started off stage, looked back but of course I wasn't following him because I was busy wiping the face of my baby and kissing it.

Then he says, "I guess you weren't listening. My name is . . . DEATH! And, Matilda Jo Summers, you will accompany me. Let's get out of here."

So, again he started off, and again I don't follow.

"I told you, you have to come with me." Now he was petulant. Then one of the men at the table, and, wait a minute, now all their faces are clear to me, crystal clear. And I never saw any of them before in my life. Anyway, one of the men said, a stocky fellow, "Do you want a smoke?" and he was looking directly at me while he held up one of these gaspers they were passing out last night. I shook my head but Death answered.

"I myself do not smoke"—then he pulled himself up proudly—"but I do not object to others smoking in my prescience."

I said something to you, something I could not hear in the audience, and you left the table, went off stage, and brought me another diaper for my baby. I smiled at you and you went back to the game.

"For some reason, you're ignoring me," said Death, "but I'm telling you now for the last time, sister, if you don't leave that baby and come with me by the time I count to three, I will take you *and* the damn baby. One . . . " and here he started off, looked back, and then stopped because of course I was busy with my baby. Mind you, I was squirming in the audience. The thought that he might take my baby was tearing me apart, but I was bound to the seat by some invisible force and couldn't yell at the other me (the real me?) on stage who simply wasn't paying any attention. I could feel that, but not where I was working on stage. "Two . . . and Three!!"

Now I was seated on a chair, a rocker, that had somehow appeared, and I was rocking my baby on my lap.

"What the hell is going on here?" Death says now. He starts to weep, and I felt for him in the audience, but not on stage. "Oh, what's the use?" Death moaned. "I'll never amount to anything. I wasn't always like this, I've had a lot of different jobs, lives. But it's my turn in the barrel and here I am and I can't even do this right.

"It's always been the same with me. I can't seem to make decisions for other people. Once in another life, I was a sixteen-year-old boy in Manchester, England and there was a big dance and I knew I couldn't take, I couldn't ask, Miss England, the one I wanted. So I went down the list of the birds I knew" (here, Toddy, he had an English North Country accent) "and I mean down to the bottom, Ethel Dahlstrom, a girl with a lot of glasses and no bosom at all. So I took a deep breath, phoned her, and said, 'I'll take you to the dance, Ethel.' And she had other plans, she did. Oh hell, what's the use of trying to make plans for others. I had made such a difficult compromise for myself and she wasn't co-operative at all, at all.

"Then another time I was a woman, not married, never married, never loved, thirty years old" (now poor old Death was crying like a baby and had a handkerchief, pure white with a black border, in his hand, wiping where his eyes were supposed to be and he was speaking in an awful voice, this poor old virgin's voice, whining, pitiful, you couldn't like her and you hated yourself for not liking her), "and some man, a very rough man, my dear, had me in his arms, holding me and kissing me with his whiskey breath and trying to unbutton my blouse; my dear, he was brutal with those hands, hands, all over me and he was saying 'You're beautiful, do you know that? You're beautiful.' And I said, 'No, I'm not beautiful. I'm attractive.' He pulled back, took a good look at me and left! Oh, I knew full well I wasn't beautiful, but I thought that if I did not aspire to being beautiful, God would then let me be at least attractive. I always wanted to be attractive, to believe I was. But I never did.

"Then I tried going into business for myself with a little company" and here Death's voice was perfectly Middle Western Rotarian, in fact I saw him playing with a watch chain that had an Elks' tooth on it. "This company doesn't happen for another sixty years or so—hold all calls, Miss M! For sixty years—so I'd appreciate your keeping this confidential—I call this firm Future Explorations, Ltd. But that was a flop too; even though I don't go into this thing for another sixty years, it was still years ahead of its time. And the big conglomerates got into it fast and Jewed all the prices down. Oh, no, that was a a flop too and here I am in the barrel again, just poor old Death. Nobody cares if I live or die."

He was crying so pitifully, Tod. And for the first time I heard and spoke with him onstage.

"I care."

"But which do you want?" he wailed. And he simply faded away.

"What do you think of that, Tod?"

"What happened to your baby? And to me and the guys?" I didn't know what the dream was telling her, but I had the feeling she was trying to tell me something.

"Oh, my baby was fine. I kept rocking her, she was on my lap. I just don't remember what happened to you and the others. Then my baby and I both went to sleep, I guess, and I woke up alone. Isn't that a nice dream?"

"Well, it has many ramifications," I said. "What do you think it means?"

"I don't think it means a goddam thing."

Leroy, tell you what I want tonight, no, now. Let me have a nice steak tartare, with the egg, capers, and all, put some of that sauce of yours on it and, let's see, bring me a chilled glass of Heineken's. That'll do it. I think I'm winding down. Never had so much fun in my life.

Everything changed, got shadowy. Matilda got very quiet, not really morose, but there just wasn't much humor there at all any more. Lilac never dropped in now and the only time I saw her, she crossed the street, got into her car, and drove away. If she had seen me, would she have stopped and talked? Would I? I'm sure Matty ran into her at the market sometime, she must have. But she never mentioned it. We never heard from Father Bob or Imogene "Call Me Gene" or Purita or Emmett Placer or Bert Larrabee.

The only one who kept coming around, gay as all get out, was Godiva and she certainly did cut the gloom. I used to think she was just one of those good-natured old whores but I realize now she had a lot more than that. I think she knew how good she was and that's why she still did it. Just because someone does something doesn't mean it's easy for them.

Meanwhile I was out selling these oil shares in my

private dust bowl, but the fun had gone out of it. I didn't get much thrill when they bought, which God knows was rare, and I didn't keep coming in like I used to when I got a jab on the nose with one of those "Well, I'm not sure." My trips took me farther and farther away because I'd used up the San Fernando Valley and environs so that I was away from home a lot and that didn't seem to make much difference to me or to Matilda. I might as well have been on a ten-to-five job for all the good my free-enterprise system was doing me.

But I did keep plugging and in these United States if you do keep plugging and you live long enough (I've done both, so far) it'll all come to you, like a bright rainbow. Then again, maybe I had no choice. Who knows. It was all dreary selling; I had about twenty per cent of the property sold off in dribs and drabs and had lost my whole appetite for the deal.

Nobody was telling me what to do any more but then nobody was telling me much of anything any more and when someone did, little ones like "You should eat here; it's great" or telephone operators with "Please hang up and dial again," it didn't bother me so much.

One night Godiva called, said Bert was out in Long Beach and could she drop in for a while, so we said fine. This was almost a year after the festivities at Emmett Placer's castle and during that time she had made Matilda her confidante so I knew that Godiva had also become Emmett's girl friend. She suspected Bert knew something but didn't want to pursue the inquiry because Emmett was like an ace in the hole for him. All that money, but he'd never put the arm on him because once he did that, if the pitch didn't work, whatever it might be, he'd lose that ace. All hustlers have one like that, for all the good it does them. She came over in the most gorgeous dark mink coat you ever saw and when she sat down she didn't even take it off. We talked politely for a couple of minutes about nothing much in particular and then she broke into one of those big hearty laughs that does fill a room with delight.

"Isn't either of you peasants going to say something about my dark expensive mink coat?"

"It's beautiful, Godiva," I said.

"Where'd you get it?" Matty got right to the point.

"I got it for my birthday," Godiva said. She had that habit you always find in people who live by their wits of answering a question but not the one you ask. I remember saying to Red Sutton once, "That's a nice-looking suit, Red. Where'd you get it?" and he answered, "I've had it for years," with the nicest smile but steely eyes, I thought at the time, as if to say he'd tell me what he wanted me to know and that I shouldn't poke my nose in other people's business or I could get it broken.

But Matilda is direct.

"Who from?" she asked.

"I got it at Jack Levin's, you know, the furrier."

"I didn't think you got it at a shoe store. But I asked who from, not where."

Godiva laughed again, took off the coat, and swept it by both of us long enough for us to feel it and then slung it with obvious carelessness on a chair.

"Well, Bert said 'What do you want for your birthday?' and so I told him 'a mink coat' because I never lie to Bert unless I have to and I didn't feel I had to at that time. He did blink once, but that was all. Then I happened to mention to Emmett, who is really a darling, that my birthday was coming up and then *he* asked me what I wanted and I blurted out 'A mink coat.' Well, there I was in a pretty pickle, which was my own fault of course, I'm not blaming anybody else. Because naturally Emmett insisted on getting me a mink coat too.

"Now Flo Levin, Jack's wife, and I danced together in fairs, years ago. So she helped me arrange things so that neither of the boys would have their feelings hurt, because I did so want to be fair to both of them and give them the pleasure of giving me the coat. I took Bert in to Jack Levin's with me first and I picked out this coat. Bert made a reasonably good price with Jack and they promised I could pick up the coat with my name embroidered in it and a couple of other things I asked for, like extra skins on the sleeve and all that, in a week. The next day Emmett and I went in and ordered the same coat and I threw my arms around him in thanks, just like I had with Bert. I got the coat a week later from Jack, who gave me back half the money he got, that is the total from Bert and Emmett. But do you know what the son of a bitch did, I found out? He told me Bert had paid a certain price they had arranged on in private and that was all and I *trusted* him. Well, my Bert paid $500 more than Jack said, I know because I inadvertently found out when I was going through Bert's desk drawer one day where his checkbook is. Naturally I went back to Jack and called him on it and got the other two fifty. He said he'd forgotten. What a chiseler!

"But anyway"—her face brightened again, she could never be angry long—"here I am with the coat, they are both happy, and I have a few dollars extra in the kitty for little old Godiva herself. Do you need any?"

"No, thank you, darling," said Matilda—too fast. But I know the Godivas better than that. They don't waste questions like that. They surround the truth.

"Why do you ask?" I said.

"Because you may. Soon."

"What's happening? What did you find out?"

"Emmett is very powerful. And very tricky. Though very sweet. But I don't always know what he's doing. Last night he had some friends over from the Treasury Department and I dropped by there since Bert was away and I was alone and so was Emmie; Bubbles is in Palm Springs. They were talking about oil leases and what some people were doing to the reputation of honest oil dealers—is that a laugh—by selling leases to land and never drilling a well. These fellows were telling Emmett that they were going to clamp down on oil-stock hustlers and he told them that was a good thing, a necessary thing and all that. Now you've got to remember that Emmett gives a lot of money to election campaigns. And then you didn't particularly endear yourself to him with that sock on the jaw and if he wanted to give any name to them, you can guess whose it would be. In fact, Toddy dear, you don't have to guess."

"Toddy, can they get you for this?" Matty was anxious, the first sign of interest in me she'd shown in a year.

"They've got me."

"You have to go there and wildcat one well, as a sign of good faith," Godiva said.

"With what? That'll cost twenty-five grand, at least." I felt sunk. And that was the first sign of life I'd felt either, in a year. But a feeling helps and it sets you going, so even if it is on the wrong path, you are at least mobile. I began thinking I had a pretty good equity in the house, didn't know how much, could find out.

"I can let you have 6,250 bucks," said Godiva, smiling.

"How the hell do you know I could pay you back?"

"I don't." Then she stopped smiling and just looked at us. "But I'm for you guys. Against all the other guys."

The next day I signed a note for $6,250 with Godiva at fifteen-per-cent interest and raised another 13,500 on the house, not enough altogether but a start and I was beginning to move again, that was the important thing. I guess I needed that picture of jail in my mind because staying out of the slammer has been the motivating force in my life. Then I called Wingy in New York to tell him the score and see if he knew anybody in Enid, Oklahoma, which was about 100 miles north of my property, who could put me on the track of how to get a well dug. I'd been selling this garbage for years but didn't know a damn thing about it. The only one he knew there was Doc Whitcomb, who years ago had a bucket shop in Chicago, where I met him a couple of times and, according to Wingy, had made one good score in Bar Harbor, Maine and now was semiretired in Enid with an organic-food and homeopathic-cure store. Doc had actually had one year of dental school, so this must be a good dodge for him, I thought, and I left L.A. full of hope.

Never should have. I got to Enid three o'clock in the afternoon and after checking into the Grand Hotel I called the number Wingy had given me. Doc had died the day before of ptomaine poisoning and the funeral was the next day.

Well, I went to the funeral to pay my respects and see who was around. There seemed to be a lot of legitimate citizens about but I heard a few of the fellows go by the coffin and then one another murmuring "Hello, Connie," which is our way of identification. So I went up to the widow, whose name actually was Connie, and introduced myself. Good-looking, strong-looking woman about sixty.

"Oh, Tod Fleedhurn, it's so nice of you to come all the way down here. You know, Doc used to talk about you a lot, he liked you so much."

"That's nice to hear, though I only met him once or twice."

"I know. But we met your mother and Preston and your mother told us so many stories about you. Why don't you come by the house this evening. We all would love to see you."

There were about a dozen of Connie's friends there that night, three or four of whom were grifters and the others just civilians and their wives. About an hour after I got there, the widow took me aside and told me that Wingy had phoned her and she asked how she could help me. So I told her and she nodded.

"Go over to the New West Bar and Grill at Thurston and Bradley tomorrow morning and see the Missout Kid; you know him, don't you?"

"Sure, from Philly. But what time will he be there?"

"He's always there and you've got to get there in the morning because he goes on the hard stuff after noon. But he knows everybody in town. Don't, for Christ's sake, tell him the whole story, just ask him to get you someone who can honcho this project."

"Right. This is awfully nice of you, Connie. I won't forget it.".

"That's all right. Just come by for dinner once in a while when you get settled. It's going to be pretty lonesome around here. I don't feel it yet, but I will, I will. You can spend forty years with the devil and miss him when he goes and Doc was no devil. He was an angel."

I spotted the Missout Kid as soon as I went into the New West Bar and Grill at ten the next morning and went over.

"Hello, Tod," he said. "Connie Whitcomb phoned this morning to tell me to help you. Have a beer."

He'd already had a few, I could tell that, and he was one of those boozers who get drunk very quick and never much worse or better. Connie was right, I had to get to him early. I tried but he kept ordering more beer and looking at the clock for the whiskey witching hour and talking about himself.

"I'll do anything for a friend of Connie Whitcomb's. She's good people. And smart. We had a Faith-Healing dodge together, but it went down the tube a couple of years ago so they opened that food store and I stayed with an astro chart I've had for years. Always had it because it was my dad's before me. That store has been a slot machine for them. Turns over $100,000 a year for practically no work and half that's profit. But I tell you, Tod, if you're looking to get into something, Faith Healing is Dead. I wouldn't put a dime into Faith Healing."

"Father Bob seems to do all right with it. But I want . . ."

"He's an exception. I'm talking about it as an industry. But this little astro chart of mine, well, like I said before, it's family so I couldn't give it up, but the little bastard throws off $70,000 in its worst year. I'm getting tired; I might let you buy into that. Also, it wouldn't be right to pack it in; a lot of people depend on it. It performs a service. 'Beware of your too generous spirit today, but the stars are right for you to engage in a business deal.' We never lose a subscriber except because of death, but we just keep adding them. Even have some now in London, England. That sheet is a license to steal."

Then I told him that I had this property south of Enid and wanted to drill there and did he know who could help me. The Missout Kid lumbered to his feet; My God how he'd changed. He used to be a good-looking, almost sleek roper but all that beer had gone to his belly and the booze had bloated his face. He was huge. Went to the phone booth and called a number and then came back and sat down.

"He'll be here in a half hour," he said.

"Who will?"

"Eddie Red Horse, that's who. The best Indian oil man in Oklahoma. He's Osage." The Kid took another swig of beer, looking over his glass at the clock again. "They're different. The others are bad Indians. The Osage are good Indians."

Eddie Red Horse showed up about a quarter past eleven so I started talking fast, before the Missout Kid went on whiskey. Eddie was a guy somewhere between forty and fifty, dark of course, wiry and with good eyes. He was astonished that I wanted to drill on that land because, he said, there had been drilling all around there with nothing but dry holes. But I told him I had had a dream about it and he seemed to buy that. He could be free to start on the project in a couple of weeks and meanwhile would line up some of the people he'd need and see about renting equipment.

"You got enough loot for all this, Tod?" asked the Missout Kid.

"I hope so. Why?"

"No reason."

"What'll it run?" I asked Eddie Red Horse.

"Hard to tell. You've got to figure twenty-five grand minimum. You've got to figure that because it'll take you down 4,000 feet. But if you don't hit there and you want to go on to 5,000 or 6,000, well hell it can all run you another twenty-five."

"That's O.K.," I said. Of course I was only going to drill for show so 25,000 should carry it all for me. But I was short about six grand even there.

Then it turned noon. The Kid let out a whoop and ordered bourbon all around. I stayed with them for a couple of hours because I thought I might find out more information about something, I didn't even know what, but then the Missout Kid got to drinking more and more, kept talking about how happy he was in the Great West where a man could get closer to nature, and to God, and have the stars as his blanket at night and every man knew his neighbor and his neighbor was his friend and "give a man a good horse between his legs and what more can he want?" and all that. In all the weeks and months I was there in Oklahoma, I never saw the Missout Kid outside that Bar and Grill.

Eddie Red Horse was a different kind of drunk. During the time I worked with him he was conscientious and bright. But when he'd get a few belts at the end of the day, he'd become one of those "white man come, buffalo go" Indians. Morose, turn into himself. He was also a knife fighter, I heard, but everybody stayed away from him when he was drinking. Anyway, I made a date to see him the next morning and I took off for my hotel from where I called Connie Whitcomb, who invited me to dinner.

"We've got a problem, Toddy, my boy," Connie said while we were polishing off the dessert. "You're short six grand and you won't be able to get started without it."

"Maybe I can scuffle around and get it."

"I wouldn't advise it." She shook her head. "I have made what is called some discreet inquiries. New man checked in with the F.B.I. headquarters in Tulsa, and he's in charge of blue-sky investigations out of Washington. He could be in Enid at any time. Your friend Mr. Emmett Placer is highly placered."

"And there's no sense my going to the banks, is there? I haven't got anything left to borrow on but my share of the land."

"Which is marked lousy, according to Eddie Red Horse. And I promise you Emmett Placer has put the kibosh in there too."

"Do you think I'm dead, Connie?"

"I don't know what to say. I can't help you because Doc cashed in all his life insurance two months ago to get into that big poker game over at the Masonic Hall and he tapped out there. So I've got nothing."

"That's terrible, Connie."

"Oh, I've got the store. I'm all right. I just can't help you."

"What poker game did he get into?"

"Toddy, don't think of that. These guys will kill you; they're all big oil men and they just have too much money. Hell, Doc could play poker with the best, but they had too much money for him. He was ahead almost a hundred grand in that game over the year he played. But when the cards turned, well, he didn't have enough to keep him. And he died on the downward turn."

"Can you get me into that game, Connie?"

"Sure, you met two of the players here last night. But honey, they'll chew you up and spit you out."

"What else can I do? I'm not looking to keep playing to win the chandelier, I just want a stake and get out of there."

She made some calls the next day and arranged for me to get into the game the following week. She insisted on waiting because she wanted to brief me on all the players, in fact Doc had kept a book on them; some good it did him. And in going over all this with her, thinking of the game, and of the F.B.I. agent waiting for me and of being fenced in at a prison, all that gave me a feeling, for the first time, of my mortality. I studied Doc's book with Connie, played out hands with her handling the parts of the other players, and just wanted to get enough money to show that goddam agent I was drilling and go home to my Matilda. I was playing for a tie, that's all, but that's what I'd always done and who does much better? It ends the same way for all of us. I was thinking all this while Connie was telling me about the players.

". . . they're all tough. They can bet fifteen grand into you with a smile because they don't care. They've got that coming in every hour. But the one to watch out for is that little Eric Jensen. That's the one you met here last night, reddish fringe of hair. Because he watches everything and he's strange, so promise me, Toddy, you won't try to do any business. No funny shuffles. Promise?"

"I promise. But what's so strange about him?"

"He's suspicious. He already has all the money in the world except eight dollars that he's working on, but he treats life as if it's all a conspiracy instead of the plot that it really is. I think people back your way would call that paranoia. Right? But all the people I've ever known who think they've been cheated, some place along the line they dance on your grave. They look at you, whoever you are, and say 'you're the one' and the next thing you know you're out of business and you don't know what happened to you or why. That's how they get so rich and powerful."

"Eric Jensen, eh?"

"Eric Jensen," she sighed. "Then while you're watching him, one of those other millionaires may hit you across the head with a wet mackerel. I don't know why I'm helping you do this. But I guess the way Placer has you set up, it's your only chance."

"Looks that way."

During the next week I had Eddie Red Horse setting up a crew for us and making plans while I worried about money. I didn't think about the F.B.I. because I picked up my man two days after this last talk with Connie. He was wearing the F.B.I. uniform, gabardine suit and snap-brim hat, and had checked into the Grand Hotel just to be close to me, I guess, to torment me. Every now and then in the lobby he would look right at me, smile a little, and shake his head slowly. The Missout Kid told me he found out through his connections that the word was out in town to issue me no credit so I had to give Eddie Red Horse good checks for everything he was doing. And although I had always been able to scuffle around for a few bob when I needed it, I couldn't do a damn thing with this watchdog around the hotel and who knows where else. Emmett Placer had me tied up like a Christmas turkey.

The poker game was held in a big private room at the Masonic Temple, which was a beautiful big mosque-like building on the way out of Enid toward my property. Two of the fellows I had met before, at Connie's, Jensen and Ed Maire, a big blond guy also about forty. The other three were all, as Connie'd warned me, oil men and were named—I never can forget this night or anybody in it—Bob Lemon, Harry Mathews, and a fellow, older than the others, named Hank Leonard, who was called Deadeye Leonard, I never did learn why.

The game was called for eight o'clock and I got there about eight-fifteen after walking around the block a couple of times; didn't want to appear anxious. They were all standing around having long drinks except Jensen, who was sitting at the table shuffling the cards. Mathews was talking. He was another big man, had straight iron-gray hair parted in the middle like an honest bartender. I learned later that he was the lawyer for all these swells and just about anyone else with money around Enid, Oklahoma.

"Well"—he laughed—"we certainly heard some funny corporate law today." I knew I was in the right place then, if they could laugh at corporate law. By the right place, I mean I'd get paid if I won. If I won. Then he saw me enter. "Looks like here's our added starter."

Ed Maire introduced me around and I apologized for being late. "No sweat," said Deadeye Leonard. "You're a friend of Emmett Placer, aren't you?"

"I've met him. Don't know you could say we were friends."

"I've never liked him much either," said Bob Lemon.

"But he's in the same line of work we're in," Jensen said. Meaning I wasn't in the club. Maybe not. But I was in the poker game.

"That's true," said Mathews. "Let's sit down."

I bought $15,000 worth of chips, about $400 less than all I had in the world after having advanced Eddie Red Horse the money he needed. I had to win at least five grand to get that well down 4,000 feet and I had to get it down that far to satisfy the man with the white beard in Washington. The other men bought ten G's around except Jensen, who got fifteen; I suddenly felt like he was gunning for me. I hoped I wasn't getting to feel persecuted like Connie said he was.

"I was a friend of Doc Whitcomb's," I said.

"Good for you," Jensen said. "And it's your deal."

I played steady but careful poker for a couple of hours, careful verging on scared; and you can't play scared poker and win. I knew these men knew all about me, that this was my case money, I mean, and of course they all had so much that they could take advantage of that. But I liked them, they were nice guys, all of them but Jensen, whom I had this goddam complex about. I thought he was watching me, to pounce. But I was watching him too. And I could tell he was more scared than I was, even with all his money. He never bet out unless he had a lock on the hand and was no great shakes as a caller, from what I could see. All I knew was that I couldn't win the way I was going and then we broke for food at eleven-thirty.

All parties went over to the groaning board where there were cold ham and roast beef, turkey and duck, and four different kinds of salads. Then a couple of waiters appeared with six tiny hot cooked grouse along with the gravy and bread crumbs. It was all laid on good and heavy.

But I had learned from the great Charley Mayfield: Never eat when you're in a high-stake poker game. It will slow your mind down maybe only half a step. But you may need that half step. So I just had a Coca-Cola.

By the time we sat down again it was after midnight. An hour and a half later I was down to about twelve five. And I knew I had to do something drastic or I'd simply get ground out. I suddenly felt good. I had made my decision. I was the best. I knew that so clearly at the time. When my chance came, I was good and ready. *The best* and ready.

Bob Lemon was on my right and he dealt me a pair of jacks, which was what we needed for openers, and three pieces of garbage. I opened for 500. The others folded till it got around to Jensen opposite me, who called and raised two grand. Bob Lemon thought a long, long time and then he came in. I raised another 5,000. Jensen's lips got real thin, thinner than usual, and he played along. Bob dropped, as I figured he would, and then he got to dealing.

"No cards," I said.

"You'll play those?" asked Bob.

"That's right." I felt confident. When you bluff, you've got to *believe* you've got the winners. Otherwise the bluffee sure as hell won't.

Jensen bought two cards. I just had to hope he didn't fill and that he believed I had a pat hand. That's all. I pushed in the remainder of my stack.

"I bet 5,000 American dollars."

Jensen stared at his hand, looked at me, back to his hand and at me again. I could feel he hadn't filled. But I didn't know if he would call my hand or not. Then I played my best card, his paranoia.

"Looks like everything happens to you, doesn't it?" I said cheerily.

"You're goddam right it does," he snarled and he threw his hand down on the table.

"Are you seeing the hand or dropping?" asked Bob, the dealer.

"I'm dropping, I'm dropping," said Jensen. "But I want to see his openers!"

I turned my hand and showed the whole five cards, including the pair of jacks.

"Goddammit, I had three aces," shouted Jensen, turning over all his cards.

"You certainly did," I said, picking up his cards and examining them closely. "And now, gentlemen, I must leave you. It's late, I have a lot of work to do in the morning, and anyway you fellows are too tough for me."

"Now what exactly does that mean?" asked Deadeye.

"It means that somebody's been fingernailing the aces in this deck. Good night, gentlemen."

What I didn't tell them was that I now had enough for my first drill and that I had marked those aces myself when I picked up Jensen's hand. I left figuring that if I set them to fighting among themselves, it would get their minds off me. Anyway, you've got to have some fun in your work.

24

I sent my winnings in to Barclays Bank in England, where I'd always kept a tiny account ever since the war, thinking it might come in useful sometime and now was the time. Because in the next month and a half we drilled down 4,000 feet and hit a rich load of dust, but by that time I had contracted a severe case of oil fever. Though I didn't have enough money, I told Eddie Red Horse to keep drilling, and between my Los Angeles bank account, the one I had opened in Enid, and Barclays, I was kiting so many checks that I felt like Ben Franklin. But I didn't care. I was on a roll. I felt it. I knew it.

There was never a strike like the Matilda Number 1. With the possible exception of Number 2 and Number 3 and Number 16 and all the others that you must have read about if you've studied the history of Fleedhurn Fields. I was rich, Big Rich. I felt good because all the widows, orphans, and pharmacists I had sold oil leases to were now going to get rich too. Not as rich as me, of course, but I'm sure they would understand that and want it that way.

By the time I got back to Los Angeles, I was feeling great, not only because of the dough but because, goddammit, I had done something, I hadn't lazed around moaning about bad breaks. I was successful because Effort is Success, anything else you get for that effort is gravy, a dividend of life. Just look around you and you'll see. Hell, I've got a Mex gardener now and he's the most successful son of a bitch I know. He's a hunchback but he's always trying. Has a big mustache and long hair now, which is the style. Wears mod clothes and you'd have thought he'd have stopped trying to look good, but never. Always trying, always planting new flowers and bushes on the estate. Some come up good, some don't. But he never quits. He steals me blind doing all this but I know that and, what the hell, I like the little greaser and what's more I can even afford him.

All this changed our relationship, Matilda's and mine. For that whole year and a half we hadn't been anything to each other. I would look around the living room and think, There's the couch and there's the chair and there's the television set and there's Matilda, and she felt the same way, I know for sure.

But when I flew back, she met me at the airport. I took her to Scandia for a big dinner with champagne and then home where we looked at each other, smiled, then broke into laughter.

"I do love you, Matty, I surely do."

"But why, Tod? A poor little ex-jumper like me."

"I love you because you're lucky."

"What makes you say I'm lucky?"

"Because you've got me, Matty."

"Whatever you say, honey. Whatever you say."

The words I've been waiting to hear all my life. Told me by a beautiful girl snuggling in my arms. Because, remember, she was my definition of beauty.

Epilogue

And that's all there is to it. I just wanted to write you this, Dad, a letter from a seventy-year-old boy to his father to show you, yes, and to demonstrate to the young people of America that when a man does his own thinking, when he learns to execute individual responsibility, and when he applies himself and works hard, the rewards are there. In my case some $84,000,000 give or take $1,000,000. I made a good deal with the oil companies with the help of Amos "Wingy" Loeffler, my old lawyer from New York who had become a big Wall Street attorney. I don't forget my old friends especially when they can do me some good and Wingy had put in four years in the Justice Department.

Interesting thing happened with Matilda and me. As we started to get big rich in a hurry, our relationship turned into battle royals. Lots more to fight about, I guess. Couldn't tell what we needed from what we wanted. Had the most awful rows full of screaming and cursing. One day on the corner of Pico and La Cienega, when I had Leroy stop the Rolls so I could get out and buy a cigar at the same time Matty thought she had to hurry to get to her hair appointment, she followed me out to the drugstore and back to the sidewalk and started to swear at me while I was lighting my cigar. There was a big truck parked there by the side of the road, back of us, and the truck driver, whose arm had the Marine Corps insigne tattooed on it, said "Lady, please, that is terrible language," and covered his ears. That set her off more. She swung her alligator pocketbook at me and it was a savage blow to my ear that could have deafened me, but luckily I had turned around to kick her in the ass when I saw her pulling her hand back.

So we went to old Wingy, told him we wanted to split up and I wanted to do the fair thing by Matty. Of course "fair" is as useless a word as "reasonable." Anyway, he showed us that the only sensible thing to do from a fiscal point of view was to get married for six months and then split because of the California community-property law. Otherwise we would have been killed by taxes. So we agreed to that.

We did finally get married. And we stayed together, barely speaking for those six months. Had this big house by then so we each took a wing. I marked off the days on a big calendar in the kitchen that she could see and she did the same thing on the one I had in my den. I almost never saw her because I rise early and she slept till noon every day: habits. I get up early because I always used to hit the road early and she still thought she was dancing around in a night club till late so she should sleep till noon. But the morning of the day the six months were up I went down to the kitchen to make myself some coffee and, lo and behold, Matilda was there, a glass of freshly squeezed orange juice at my place at the table and the smell of good coffee in the room. It took me back to the first night we'd spent together in New York.

"Do you want your eggs over easy or straight up?"

Matty asked. I didn't know she could even find the grocery store.

"Straight up."

"Bacon crisp?"

"Absolutely." I did feel good, but I had to bring up the point. "Well, honey, today's the day we file."

"File what, darling?" She put some lightly buttered toast down.

"Well, for divorce. The six months are up."

"Oh, Toddy. Why can't two grown people sit down and discuss these things like two grown people?" Then came the eggs and some Tiptree Farm Little Scarlet Strawberry Jam. Goddam little broad, she must have been planning this, must have ordered that jam from Jurgensen's Fancy Groceries days before, because I hadn't been able to find it anywhere else in Los Angeles. "You know you don't want a divorce any more than I do."

"Well," I said weakly, "I've never had one."

"And all our friends have them." She put her arm around me and kissed me on the cheek while I was shoveling some egg in.

"Well, let's be our own unique family. What the hell do you say?"

What could I say? If she needed me, she needed me. And at that moment I wouldn't have let her go for anything in the world. I took her into the den after a second cup of coffee and gave her the vacuum cleaner I had hidden there, locked in the closet, that I promised her fifteen years ago along with that diamond ring you can see on her finger that I had bought from Feather Finger Freddie downtown in anticipation of such a thing happening that morning.

And here's the best part. We've applied to adopt a Vietnam war baby orphan and we're to get it this week.

My darling's dream is going to come true and I will be playing cards in the corner with my pals who will be trying to hustle me out of some of my scratch. They will have some case.

The baby will grow up great. You will be proud. I've always been.